The Struggle for Sea Power

The Struggle for Sea Power
by M. B. Synge

©2008 Wilder Publications

Wilder Publications, LLC.
PO Box 3005
Radford VA 24143-3005

ISBN 10: 1-60459-496-9
ISBN 13: 978-1-60459-496-6

The Story of the Great Mogul

"Oh, East is East, and West is West, and never the twain shall meet."
—KIPLING.

The wonderful story of England's conquest of India reads, even to-day, like some fairy legend of the Old World.

It is the story of how one small island, away in the Northern seas, conquered an empire ten times its own size, at a distance of 6000 miles. In the ages of long ago, when the Egyptians were building their pyramids, when the Phœnicians were sailing to the Pillars of Hercules, when the Greeks were adorning Athens and the Romans were spreading their empire far and wide, this England was still sleeping on the waves of the boundless sea.

It was not till after the Roman Empire had fallen, not till the Portuguese had found their way across the Sea of Darkness to India, not till the Spaniards had discovered the New World, that England awoke to a sense of the great possibilities that lay before her. Slowly and surely, from this time onwards, she stretched forth her arms over the broad seas that had once been her barriers, until, by her untiring energy, she won for herself an empire "on which the sun never sets."

Her first great conquest was that of India or Hindostan—the land of the Hindoos. It is a country cut off from Asia by a lofty range of mountains known as the Hima-laya, or snow abode. Here are some of the highest peaks in the world, never scaled by man. Here, too, rise the largest rivers in India—the Indus and the Ganges, on which most of the large towns are built. Most of the country lies within the tropics. Hence it is a land of wondrous starlight and moonlight, a land of whirlwind and tempest, of pitiless sun and scorching heat. Here to-day, as of old, are men with dark faces and long beards, dressed in turbans and flowing robes—men for the most part Mohammedans, praying at intervals throughout the day, with their faces toward Mecca.

At the time that Alexander the Great entered India,—327 years before the birth of Christ,—the land was parcelled out into a number of small kingdoms, each under the government of its own Raja. Each Raja had a council known as the Durbar. When a Raja conquered other Rajas he was known as a Maha-raja or Great Raja, and all these words are used in India to-day.

In the sixteenth century a race of Mongols or Moguls swept into India from Central Asia and founded an empire in the north. Marco Polo had heard a great deal about these Mongols when he was at the court of the Great Khan. The first of the Mogul emperors was called Baber, or the Tiger; but he was succeeded by a yet more famous grandson called Akbar, whose power is spoken of still in India to-day. Akbar added to the Mogul Empire until it became the most extensive and splendid empire in the world. In no European kingdom was so large a population subject to a single ruler, or so large a revenue poured into the treasury. The beauty and magnificence of the buildings, the huge retinues and gorgeous decorations, dazzled the eyes of those accustomed to the pomps of Versailles.

But under the Great Mogul Aurangzeb, the "Conqueror of the Universe," the empire reached the height of its glory. He had usurped the throne, put his father into prison, and murdered his three brothers. His crown was uneasy, but secure. At Delhi he held his magnificent court. Here was the palace of the Great Mogul, built on the river Jumna, a tributary of the Ganges. The magnificent gateway of the palace was guarded by two huge elephants of stone, each bearing the colossal statue of a Raja warrior on his back. Here too was the grand hall of audience, where the Durbar was held. The ceiling was of white marble, supported by thirty marble columns, bearing an inscription in gold: "If there be a Paradise on earth, it is this." The throne was in a recess at the back of the hall, and over the throne was a peacock made of gold and jewels, valued at a million pounds.

One day Aurangzeb was sitting on his throne at a Durbar at Delhi, when his old tutor appeared before him. The Great Mogul had suddenly stopped his pension, and he had come to know the reason. Aurangzeb gave him the explanation in public.

"This tutor," he cried, "taught me the Koran (Mohammedan Bible) and wearied me with rules of Arabic grammar, but he told me nothing at all of foreign countries. I learnt nothing of the Ottoman Empire in Africa. I was made to believe that Holland was a great empire, and that England was bigger than France."

When his birthday came round the Great Mogul was weighed in state, and if he was found to weigh more than on the preceding year there were great public rejoicings. All the chief people in the empire came to make their offerings: precious stones, gold and silver, rich carpets, camels, horses, and elephants were presented to him. He had tents of red velvet embroidered in gold. He had seven splendid thrones,—one covered with diamonds, one with rubies, one with pearls, one with emeralds, though the Peacock Throne was the most valuable. While the Great Mogul was on his throne, fifteen horses stood ready on either side, their bridles enriched with precious stones. Elephants were trained to kneel down before the throne and do reverence with their trunks. The Emperor's favourite elephant was fed on good meat, with plenty of sugar and brandy.

Aurangzeb himself was nearly one hundred years old when he died. Suspicion lest his sons should subject him to the fate which he had inflicted on his own father left him a solitary old man. As death approached terror and remorse seized him. "Come what may," he cried desperately at the last, "I have launched my vessel on the waves. Farewell! farewell! farewell!"

So passed the last of the Great Moguls who ruled for over two hundred years in India. The empire was soon after broken up, and the way left clear for England to found her great Eastern Empire beyond the seas.

Robert Clive

"Clive kissed me on the mouth and eyes and brow,
Wonderful kisses, so that I became
Crowned above Queens—a withered beldame now
Brooding on ancient fame."
—KIPLING (Madras).

During the forty years after the death of Aurangzeb a great change passed over India. The great Mogul Empire was broken up; enemies invaded the land from north and south. They preyed on the defenceless country, they marched through the gates of Delhi and bore away in triumph the Peacock Throne and all its priceless jewels.

From the time of Alexander the Great little intercourse had been held between Europe and the East. But from that May day in 1498, when Vasco da Gama and his brave Portuguese sailors stepped ashore at Calicut, there was constant communication with the ports on the western coast. For some time Portugal had claimed exclusive right to her Indian trade, but after a time Dutch ships sailed to her eastern ports. The enterprise of Holland roused commercial enthusiasm in England and France until these three nations had established trading stations in the East.

The Dutch headquarters was at Batavia; the French at Pondicherry, on the east coast of India; the English at Madras, some eighty miles to the north. The governor of Pondicherry was a Frenchman called Dupleix. He was the first European to see the possibility of founding an empire on the ruins of the Great Mogul, though it was reserved for the English to carry out his wonderful idea.

Neither the French nor the English traders knew much about the government of India at this time. They knew that they paid a yearly rent to the native ruler or Nawab, who lived in Oriental splendour at the city of Arcot, some sixty-five miles west of Madras. This Nawab of Arcot was in his turn under the Nizam of Hyderabad, and both in the old days were under the Great Mogul.

Dupleix, full of his dreams of empire, saw that his first step must be to capture the English trading station of Madras. England and France were at war, so he seized this opportunity of attacking Madras, which was but poorly defended, and carried off the English in triumph to Pondicherry. Here all was joy and gladness. Salutes were fired from the batteries, Te Deums were sung in the churches. The Nizam came to visit his new allies. Dupleix, dressed in Mohammedan garments, entered Pondicherry with him, and in the pageant that followed took precedence of the native court. He was declared Governor of India from Hyderabad to Cape Comorin, a country the same size as France itself; he was given command of seven thousand men; he ruled over thirty millions of people with absolute power, and the Nizam himself became but a tool in his hands.

It was at this moment that the genius and valour of a single young Englishman, Robert Clive, changed the whole aspect of affairs, and won the empire of India for England.

"Clive," said a Frenchman afterwards, "understood and applied the system of Dupleix."

Robert Clive was the eldest of a large English family. He was born in Shropshire in the year 1725. At a very early age he showed that he had a strong will and a fiery passion, "flying out on every trifling occasion." The story is still told in the neighbourhood of how "Bob Clive," when quite a little boy, climbed to the top of a lofty steeple, and with what terror people saw him seated on a stone spout near the top. He was sent from school to school, but made little progress with his learning. Instead, he gained the character of being a very naughty little boy. True, one far-seeing master prophesied that he would yet make "a great figure in the world," but for the most part he was held to be a dunce. Nothing was expected from such a boy, and when he was eighteen his parents sent him off to India, in the service of the East India Company, to "make his fortune or die of a fever."

His voyage was unusually long and tedious, lasting over a year. At last he arrived at the port of Madras—a barren spot beaten by a raging surf—to find himself very lonely and very poor in a strange land. He found some miserably paid work in an office, but he was shy and proud and made no friends. Moreover, the hot climate made him ill.

"I have not enjoyed one happy day since I left my native land," he cried piteously. Twice, in desperation, the poor home-sick boy tried to shoot himself, but twice he failed.

"Surely," he cried at the second failure—"surely I am reserved for something great."

So it happened that Robert Clive was at Madras when the French came and carried away the English captives to Pondicherry. Disguising themselves as natives, in turbans and flowing robes, Clive and some friends managed to escape to another English trading station. There was no more office work to be done at present, and Clive, together with hundreds of other Englishmen, entered the army to fight against the French. His bravery and courage soon raised him above his fellows, and he became a captain.

Clive was now twenty-five. He saw plainly that unless some daring blow were aimed at the French soon, Dupleix would carry all before him. He suggested a sudden attack on Arcot, the residence of the Nawab; and though the scheme seemed wild to the point of madness, he was given command of 200 Europeans and some native troops to march against the town.

Arcot was sixty-five miles away. The fort was known to be garrisoned by 1100 men, but Clive marched bravely forth. During the march a terrific storm arose. The rain swept down in a deluge on the little army, the lightning played around them, the thunder pealed over their heads; but they pushed on through it all, undaunted in their desperate undertaking. Tidings of their fearless endurance reached the town before them. A panic seized the native garrison: they abandoned the fort. Not a shot was fired, and Clive with his 500 men entered the city in triumph. The young boy-captain had already won a deathless renown.

The Black Hole of Calcutta

"Clive it was gave England India."
—BROWNING.

It was not likely that the spirited little army should be left in undisputed possession of Arcot, and Clive now prepared for an inevitable siege. Soon 10,000 men had swarmed into the place, hemming in the garrison on every side. Days grew to weeks, and the ready resource of Clive alone saved the situation. The handful of men—European and native—caught the spirit of their leader, and each became a hero. History contains no more touching instance of native fidelity than that related of the men who came to Clive, not to complain of their own scanty fare, but to propose "that all the grain should be given to Europeans, who required more nourishment than the natives of Asia. The thin gruel, strained away from the rice, would do for them," they said. With such as these Clive held the fort for fifty days.

At last the French resolved to storm the town. Clive busied himself with preparations. In the evening he threw himself down to sleep, utterly tired out; but he was soon awakened, and at his post in a moment. The French attacked in strong force. They had brought with them huge elephants, with great pieces of iron fixed on their foreheads, to try and break down the gates. The English fired on them; and the unhappy creatures, unused to firearms, turned round and fled in their fright into the midst of the French, trampling many under foot. Night fell, and Clive, with his little band of weary men, passed an anxious time. Morning dawned to find the enemy had melted away. The siege of Arcot was ended. The growing power of the French in India was arrested. Robert Clive was the hero of the hour.

Indeed, not long after this Dupleix was recalled from the East by Louis XV., his dream of empire ended, to die in France heart-broken.

But India's troubles were by no means at an end. English trade in the East was growing, and the English had long ago established a trading station at Calcutta on the river Hoogly, one of the mouths of the Ganges. They had had no water-way at Madras; but here, at Calcutta, they had been able to penetrate inland and annex some of the surrounding country, known as Bengal.

Now the Nawab of Bengal hated the English. His imagination was fired with fabulous stories of the vast wealth stored up in the treasury at Calcutta. So he collected a huge army, and in the year 1756 he appeared on the outskirts of the town. The English were taken by surprise,—they had no Clive to lead them to victory,—and the Nawab took Calcutta with ease, making 146 prisoners. But the treasury did not yield the vast riches he had been led to expect, and he wreaked his revenge on the luckless prisoners. It was a hot night in June when the 146 English captives were driven by clubs and swords into a little room some twenty feet square, with only two small gratings at the entrance to let in air. The "Black Hole" had been built to shut up troublesome soldiers: it was intended to hold four or five at a time. To cram in 146 human beings was to court slow but certain death. The day had been fiercely hot, the night was sultry and stifling. Not a breath of air could enter to relieve the sufferings of the Europeans, too tightly packed into the small space to move. In vain they cried for mercy; in vain they appealed to the guards in their agony. The guards only replied from outside that the Nawab was asleep, and none dared wake him or remove a single prisoner without his leave. Then followed cries for water. A few water-skins were brought to the gratings, but in the mad struggle to reach it many were trampled to death. The heartless guards only held burning torches to the gratings and mocked at their frantic struggles. As the long night passed away the struggles ceased, the screams died away, and a few low moans were the only sounds audible. Morning dawned at last. The Nawab awoke and ordered the doors to be opened. Twenty-three fainting people alone staggered forth: the rest lay dead in heaps upon the floor. And even to-day, though nearly 150 years have passed away since that horrible crime, the Black Hole of Calcutta cannot be mentioned without a shudder.

The tale of horror thrilled through the British Empire. All eyes turned to the young hero of Arcot to avenge the wrongs done to his countrymen, and Robert Clive was soon hurrying to the scene of action.

Early in January he arrived at Calcutta, and soon the British flag was waving above the town. Meanwhile the Nawab was waiting for him at Plassey, some ninety-six miles to the north of Calcutta, with a tremendous army, at least twenty times the size of Clive's. Clive was marching north, hoping for help to be sent, but he reached the banks of the Hoogly with a force wholly inadequate for the work before him. He was in a painfully anxious dilemma. Before him lay a wide river, across which, if things went ill, not one would ever return. For the first time in his life he shrank from the fearful responsibility of making up his mind. He was but thirty-two at the time. He called a council of war. Should they attack the mighty force before them with their little band of men, or wait for help?

"Wait for help," said the officers; and Clive himself agreed with them.

But still he was not satisfied. He retired alone under the shade of a tree near by, and spent an hour in the deepest thought. Then he returned to the camp. He knew his mind now: he was determined to risk everything. "Be in readiness to attack to-morrow," he cried.

The river was soon crossed, and Clive with his army took up his quarters in a grove of mango-trees, within a mile of the enemy. He could not sleep. All night long he heard the sound of drums and cymbals from the vast camp of the Nawab. He knew but too well the fearful odds against which he would fight on the morrow.

The day broke—"the day which was to decide the fate of India."

An hour after the battle began, all was over. The Nawab had mounted a camel and was in full flight, and the great native army was retreating in wild disorder. Clive stood triumphant on the battlefield of Plassey. With a loss of twenty-two men he had scattered an army of nearly 60,000, and subdued an empire larger than Great Britain. The "heaven-born general" was conqueror not only of the battlefield of Plassey, but of the British Empire in India.

The Struggle for North America

"Few, few were they whose swords of old
Won the fair land in which we dwell,
But we are many, we who hold
The grim resolve to guard it well."
—BRYANT.

"It was the volley fired by a young Virginian in the backwoods of America
that set the world on fire."

So said the great English minister Horace Walpole. Let us see why that volley
was fired.

While the English and French were fighting for the mastery of India away
in the East, a great struggle was going on between the same two peoples—New
England and New France—for the mastery of North America in the Far West.
Clive had fought till the English flag waved over the cities of Madras and
Calcutta. Now Wolfe was to fight in America till the English flag waved from
the capitals of Quebec and Montreal.

At present the lilies of France floated over these towns. They had floated
there since the early days when the first Frenchman—Jacques Cartier broke the
solitude of this distant wilderness. Canada was the seat of French power in
North America. French Canadian life centred round Quebec and Montreal, on
the banks of the river St Lawrence. Here, in the castle of St Louis, upon the
famous rock of Quebec, sat the all-powerful governor of Louis XV., King of
France. A new governor had recently been sent out—a man who viewed his
country's prospects in America with the keenest anxiety. He knew full well the
rivalry that existed between France and England in that land of the Far West.
The English had already viewed with distrust the long arms stretched out by
France over the fur-bearing regions around Hudson's Bay.

But it was in the south that the coming storm was now brewing; it was to the
south that the French governor was looking with those dreams of empire that
inspired Dupleix to conquer Southern India.

From the Canadian lakes southwards stretched a dense "ocean of foliage,"
broken only by the white gleam of the broad rivers Ohio and Mississippi. The
beautiful valleys formed by these large rivers reached to the French settlement
of New Orleans, on the Gulf of Mexico. At distant intervals, faint wreaths of

smoke marked an Indian village: otherwise all was solitude. The country was unclaimed, for the most part, by either French or English.

Now these two rivers, the Ohio and Mississippi, practically cut North America in two. A cork dropped into the small stream that rises near Lake Erie, not far from the Falls of Niagara, would flow out through the mouth of the Mississippi at New Orleans into the Gulf of Mexico.

On the sea side of these rivers lay the thirteen English colonies, fronting the broad Atlantic Ocean. These colonies were under no one local governor: each was independent, the only tie holding them together being their allegiance to the mother country. Each colony had started life on its own account. There were the colonies founded by the Pilgrim Fathers, by the Puritans, by the Quakers. There were colonies of English, Irish, and Scotch, and each colony had its own governor. Thus the English possessions at this time consisted of a long straggling line of little quarrelling Commonwealths, resting along the sea-coast between the Atlantic and the Ohio river and Alleghany mountains. Both France and England now claimed the Ohio valley, and there was little doubt that some day their respective claims must be settled by the sword. No treaty could touch such debatable ground; no one could adjust the undefined boundary in this far-distant land.

One day, in the summer of 1749, the French governor started a small expedition to explore the country about the river Ohio. It was the first of many such. Slowly but steadily the French pushed farther and farther down the valley of the Ohio. They built fort after fort, until suddenly the governor of the English colony of Virginia became aware of what was happening.

He selected a young Virginian, George Washington, to go and protest against such encroachment. He was to march to the last new French fort, with a note from his English governor, expressing a hope that the French would at once retire from British territory, and so maintain the harmony at present existing between the two countries.

It was late autumn; but George Washington pushed manfully through the dripping forests with his little band of men, till he reached the fort. He delivered his message, and started home with the first formal note of defiance from France to England. After a three months' absence and numerous hairbreadth escapes, young Washington rode into Virginia with his ominous message from the French.

There was danger ahead. The French were pushing their dreams of empire too far. The Governor of Virginia exerted himself more vigorously. He too would build forts on the Ohio. In the early spring of 1754, a little band of Virginians was sent to build a fort in a spot where two large streams meet to form the river Ohio, a spot to become famous later as the site of the city of Pittsburg. But the French were there already, and they soon tumbled the forty Virginians back again into their English settlements. Washington was now sent with 150 men to the French fort on the Ohio. He was marching on through the pathless wilderness, when news reached him that the French were advancing to clear the English out of the country.

Taking forty men, Washington groped his way through a pitch-dark soaking night to the quarters of a friendly Indian chief. The news he found was but too true. There was not a moment to be lost. At daybreak he stole forth and found the French lying in a ravine. He gave orders to fire. A volley was given by his men and returned by the French. Their commander was slain, and the French were all taken prisoners.

And so the war began.

"It was," as Horace Walpole had said—"It was the volley fired by a young Virginian in the backwoods of America that set the world on fire."

George Washington, Soldier and Patriot

"Washington—the perfect citizen."
—EMERSON.

The "young Virginian" spoken of by Horace Walpole was destined to do great things for England in America. The stories of his boyhood shadow forth his wonderful career.

George Washington was born on February 22, 1732, in a little farmhouse on the Potomac river in Virginia. His great-grandfather had sailed over to America in the days of Oliver Cromwell, and his father was now a successful landowner. The eldest son, Lawrence, was sent to England to be educated, but George was taught by the village sexton at home. He led a free open-air life, playing in the meadows, and grew up to be a manly and truthful boy.

One day his father gave him a hatchet, and the little boy had carelessly tried its edge on the bark of a young English cherry-tree which was much valued by his father. The bark was injured, and Mr Washington was seriously displeased, and began to question the servants as to who could have done such a thing.

"I did it, father," suddenly said George, looking him straight in the face and holding out the hatchet, which he knew he must forfeit; "I did it with my new hatchet."

"Come to my arms, brave boy," said his father, drawing George to him; "I would rather every tree I possess were killed, than that you should deceive me."

When he was about eight years old the big brother Lawrence returned from England, and soon a very strong friendship had sprung up between the two brothers. Not long after his return to Virginia he volunteered for service in the West Indies, and George saw him depart, in his soldier's uniform, to the martial sound of drum and fife, with a heavy heart. But a martial spirit had been aroused in the boy, and from this time forward his favourite occupation was playing at soldiers. A stick or broom-handle served for gun or sword, the meadow by the river was the battlefield, and George Washington was always the commander-in-chief. He was a good-looking boy, tall and straight, athletic and muscular. He bore a high character at home and also at school.

"George has the best writing-book in the school," his master used to say.

After his death, among his papers was found an old copy-book—which must have been written about this time—in a quaint schoolboy handwriting. It was called "Rules for Behaviour in Company and Conversation," and there were no less than one hundred of these rules carefully copied out. Here are a few of them:—

"Speak not evil of the absent, for it is unjust."

"Undertake not what you cannot perform, but be careful to keep your promise."

"Show not yourself glad at the misfortune of another, though he were your enemy."

"Make no show of taking delight in your victuals; feed not with greediness, lean not on the table, neither find fault with what you eat."

"Labour to keep alive in your breast that little spark of celestial fire called Conscience."

After his father's death in 1743, George went to live with his beloved brother Lawrence, who was now married and living at Mount Vernon in Virginia. Here he rode and hunted, helped to survey the surrounding country, and heard much talk of the disputed boundary between the French and English possessions in North America. War was in the air.

Virginia was now divided into military districts. At the age of nineteen George Washington found himself in command of one of these. So capable a soldier did he become, that, two years later, he was the "young Virginian" selected by the Governor of Virginia to carry his message a thousand miles across country to the French. The story of how he delivered that message, and its answer, has already been told.

From this time, George Washington was a marked man and a public character. His name was known in the Court at Paris as well as in London, and it was to him the Virginians now looked to help them in their troubles. They did not look in vain: Washington was one of the greatest men America ever produced. His greatness did not consist so much in his intellect, in his skill, or in his genius, but in his honour, his utter truthfulness, his high sense of duty. He left behind him, when he died, one of the greatest treasures of his country, the example of a stainless life—of a great, honest, pure and noble character— a model for his nation to form themselves by in all time to come.

"No nobler figure ever stood in the forefront of a nation's life." He was, as Emerson, the great American thinker, had said, a "perfect citizen." He was, as a fellow-citizen said after his death in 1799, "The man first in war, first in peace, and first in the hearts of his fellow-citizens."

How Pitt Saved England

"If England to itself do rest but true."
—SHAKSPERE.

When war was formally declared between France and England in 1756, it seemed as if the dreams of a French empire in America might indeed be realised. Louis XV. of France had sent the Marquis de Montcalm to press the boundary claims of Canada, and soon a long chain of forts threatened to cut off the English coast colonies from any possibility of extending their lands in any direction. The colonies themselves were hopelessly divided, and, so far, England had not awakened to a sense of her great responsibilities with regard to her empire beyond the seas.

Besides this, there were constant alarms of a French invasion on her own shores. An English fleet had just retreated before the French; Minorca, the key to the Mediterranean, had fallen into the hands of France; while Dupleix was apparently founding a French empire in India.

A despair without parallel in history took hold of English statesmen.

"We are no longer a nation," cried one English minister.

He did not know that England was on the eve of her greatest triumphs in America as well as in India. It was this dark hour that called forth the genius of William Pitt, afterwards Earl of Chatham, one of the greatest statesmen England ever had. He was the son of a wealthy governor of Madras. He had sat in Parliament for twenty-two years before his chance came.

"In England's darkest hour, William Pitt saved her."

"I want to call England out of that enervate state in which twenty thousand men from France can shake her," he said as he took office. He soon "breathed his own lofty spirit into the country he served. He loved England with an intense and personal love. He believed in her power, her glory, her public virtue, till England learnt to believe in herself. Her triumphs were his triumphs, her defeats his defeats. Her dangers lifted him high above all thought of self or party spirit."

"Be one people: forget everything but the public. I set you the example," he cried with a glow of patriotism that spread like infection through the country.

"His noble figure, his flashing eye, his majestic voice, the fire and grandeur of his eloquence, gave him a sway over the House of Commons far greater than any other Minister possessed."

"I know that I can save the country, and I know no other man can," he had said confidently.

This was the man who now turned his eyes westwards and won for his country Canada, which is hers to-day. He saw that if the English colonies in America were to be saved from the French, the mother country must save them. He appealed to the very heart of England, and by his earnestness and eloquence he changed his despairing country into a state of enthusiasm and ardour. He now made plans for the American campaign of 1758. A blow should be struck at the French in America, at three separate points. The French forts of Duquesne and Ticonderoga were to be captured, while the great French naval station Louisburg, on Cape Breton Island, beyond Nova Scotia, was to be taken. It commanded the mouth of the river St Lawrence, and no English ships could reach the capital, Quebec.

The genius of Pitt showed itself in his choice of the man selected for this difficult piece of work.

James Wolfe, the future hero of Quebec, had fought at the battle of Dettingen when only sixteen, and distinguished himself at Culloden Moor. He was now given supreme command of the expedition to the famous fortress of Louisburg, the key to Canada, which he was to conquer triumphantly.

All England now thrilled with the coming struggle in America. The merchant at his desk, the captain on the deck of his ship, the colonel at the head of his regiment,—all felt the magic influence of William Pitt. All eyes were strained towards the backwoods of the wild West, where the drama was to be played out.

Fort Duquesne was taken from the French, and to-day, on the same site, stands the city named after Pitt,—Pittsburg, one of the largest towns in Pennsylvania.

So Pitt had roused England to a sense of her danger and her responsibility, and helped her to rise to a greatness far surpassing the dreams of either Elizabeth or Cromwell.

The Fall of Quebec

"They have fallen
Each in his field of glory. Wolfe upon the lap
Of smiling victory, that moment won."
—COWPER.

Wolfe left England late in February 1759, but the winds being contrary and the seas running high, May had opened before the wild coast of Nova Scotia was dimly seen through whirling mists of fog. The Louisburg harbour was still choked with ice, and it was not till June that the advanced squadron of the fleet could begin the passage of the St Lawrence. Wolfe had never seen Quebec, the city he was sent out to capture; but he knew that Montcalm, the French general, had four times as many troops as he had, and he spared no pains to make his own troops as efficient as possible.

"If valour can make amends for want of numbers, we shall succeed," he wrote to Pitt at home. Enthusiasm soon spread through the troops. "British colours on every French fort, post, and garrison in America," they cried, as they sailed cautiously along the lower reaches of the St Lawrence river towards their goal. It seemed incredible to the French in Canada that an English fleet should navigate its way through the difficult channels of the river St Lawrence; and they received the news that the English had landed on the shores of the Isle of Orleans with surprise and dismay.

"Canada will be the grave of the British army," they said confidently; "and the walls of Quebec will be decorated with British heads."

It was June 26 when the fleet anchored at the Isle of Orleans, and beheld for the first time the rock city of Quebec. The bravest British heart might well have quailed at the sight. High up against the western sky it stood, perched on its rocky throne. The rugged outline of batteries, bristling with cannon, seemed to frown defiance at the mere handful of Englishmen, now looking across the waters at it for the first time.

"I will be master of Quebec if I stay here till the end of November," Wolfe had said.

The task before him seemed wellnigh hopeless, yet his gallant heart never despaired. He would perform this last service if it were possible. He seized Point Levi, exactly opposite the city of Quebec. This gave him complete command of the river mouth. From here, too, his troops could fire across on to the city, and he might destroy it if he failed to capture it.

Meantime Montcalm kept rigidly within the walls of Quebec. He knew that a hard Canadian winter, with its frost and snow, must compel Wolfe to retreat.

So July came and went. Daring feats were performed on both sides, but Quebec remained uncaptured by the British forces. One day the French chained some seventy ships together, filled them with explosives, and set the whole on fire. Down the river, towards the English fleet, came this roaring mass of fire, until the courageous British sailors dashed down upon it and broke it into fragments.

August arrived, with storms and cold. Fever took hold of Wolfe. Always frail in body, he lay for a time between life and death, his "pale face haggard with lines of pain and anxiety." But he struggled back to life, and planned his great attack on Quebec.

In one of his many expeditions he had discovered a tiny cove, now called Wolfe's Cove, five miles beyond Quebec. Here was a zigzag goat-path up the steep face of the towering cliff, which was over 250 feet high at this point. Wolfe had made up his mind. Up this mere track, in the blackness of the night, he resolved to lead his army to the attack on Quebec. He kept his plans to himself.

The night arrived: it was September 12.

"Officers and men will remember what their country expects of them," he cried, as he gave his troops the final orders.

It was one of the most daring exploits in the world's history.

At two o'clock at night the signal to start was given. From the Isle of Orleans, from Point Levi, the English boats stole out in the silence and darkness of the summer night. Wolfe himself was leading. As the boats rowed silently through the darkness on this desperate adventure, Wolfe repeated some lines recently written by the poet Gray,—

"The boast of heraldry, the pomp of power,
And all that beauty, all that wealth e'er gave,
Await alike the inevitable hour.
The paths of glory lead but to the grave."

"Gentlemen," he said to the officers with him in the boat, "I would rather have written that poem than take Quebec."

Suddenly the voice of a sentry at the top of the cliff challenged them.

"Who goes there?"

"The French," sang out a Highlander who had served in the foreign wars and picked up a little French.

"From which regiment?" asked the suspicious sentry.

"From the Queen's," answered the ready Highlander in French.

A convoy of provisions was expected, and the sentry let them pass. But it was a narrow escape for the British fleet stealing stealthily along under the enemy's lines. At last the cove was reached in safety. The soldiers began to climb in single file up the face of the steep cliff. Wolfe was among the first, weakened though he was with fever and anxiety. It was an anxious time. Like a chain of ants the men crawled up the steep cliff in the darkness, until, with the first streak of dawn piercing the darkness, Wolfe and his troops stood triumphantly at the top. When morning broke Montcalm was greeted with the news that the British commander, whom he had kept at bay for months, now stood with an army of 4500 men in line of battle on the plains of Abraham, overlooking Quebec. Never a word of dismay uttered the French general as he mustered his troops to defend their city against the English.

He had some 10,000 men. By nine o'clock all was ready. The battle began. In fifteen minutes it was all over. The French opened fire on the English lines at a distance of 200 yards. The English had been told by Wolfe to reserve their fire, and the men now stood with shouldered arms, as if on parade. Silent and motionless they stood amid the rain of French bullets and the din of French cheers. Then came the order to fire. Since the invention of gunpowder never had such a tremendous volley been delivered. The sudden explosion of 4000 muskets sounded like the blast of a single cannon-shot. As the smoke lifted, the French could be seen lying dead in heaps. Then Wolfe sprang forward, at the head of his men, sword in hand, and the whole line advanced. At that moment the sun burst forth, lighting up the gleaming bayonets and flashing swords. Another moment and Wolfe fell, hit by two bullets.

"Don't let my gallant soldiers see me fall," he gasped to the few men who rushed to help him.

They carried him in their arms to the rear, and laid him on the ground. They mentioned a surgeon.

"It is needless," he whispered; "it is all over with me."

The little sorrowing group stood silently round the dying man. Suddenly one spoke.

"They run! See how they run!"

"Who run?" murmured Wolfe, awaking as if from sleep.

"The enemy, sir," was the answer.

A flash of life returned to Wolfe. He gave his last military order. Then turning on his side, he whispered, "God be praised, I now die in peace."

That night, within the ruined city of Quebec, lay Montcalm mortally wounded.

"How long have I to live?" he asked painfully.

"Twelve hours possibly," they answered him.

"So much the better," murmured the defeated and dying man; "I shall not live to see the surrender of Quebec."

So the two leaders died,—one at the moment of victory, the other in the hour of defeat. If France was grieved at Montcalm's failure, all England was intoxicated with joy at Wolfe's magnificent victory. The country flamed into illuminations, for the English colonies in America were saved. French power in the Far West was crushed as it had been in the East, and "the whole nation rose up and felt itself the stronger for Wolfe's victory."

"The Great Lord Hawke"

"When the battle rages loud and long,
And the stormy winds do blow."
—CAMPBELL

The French had been beaten by the English in the East and in the West by land. Now they were to be beaten again by the English, this time by sea, and off their own coast. France was threatening an invasion of England, when Sir Edward Hawke was given command of an English fleet, with orders to blockade the French fleet and destroy the ships if possible.

How, through wild storms and tempests, the English sailor kept his dogged watch, and how, finally, he destroyed the fleet with "heroic daring," and by so doing saved his country, is one of the most thrilling stories in history.

Born in the year 1705, Hawke had been at sea ever since he was a small boy.

"Would you like to be a sailor, Ned?" he had been asked.

"Certainly, sir," the boy had answered quickly.

"Are you willing to go now, or to wait till you are bigger?"

"This instant, sir," replied the little hero.

His mother grieved bitterly over his departure from home.

"Good-bye, Ned," she said, with difficulty controlling herself. "I shall expect you soon to be a captain."

"A captain," replied the boy with derision; "Madam, I hope you will soon see me an admiral."

He rose quickly in the service. More than once he distinguished himself in sea-fights. He had more than fulfilled the traditions of the British navy, lately disgraced by the behaviour of the British Admiral Byng, who for the loss of Minorca had been tried and shot on the deck of his own ship.

Pitt had chosen Wolfe to carry out his plans at Quebec; he now chose Hawke to sail against the French, and so frustrate the threatened invasion of England.

It was in the middle of May 1759 that Hawke hoisted his flag and sailed from Torbay, to fulfil his difficult task. The French fleet, under Conflans, the ablest of French commanders, was lying snugly in the well-sheltered harbour of Brest, while more ships lay to the south at the mouth of the Loire. Hawke was to block all the ships in the harbour of Brest, and prevent their joining the others. He sailed over to the French coast, and there for six months he doggedly blockaded the French fleet. But it was a stormier season than usual. His officers and men died of disease, the bottoms of the ships grew foul, the vessels were battered by autumn gales and knocked about by the high rolling seas from the Bay of Biscay. Still the British sailor stuck to his post. Autumn drew on. Again and again the wild north-west gales drove him from his blockading ground at the mouth of the harbour of Brest; again and yet again he fought his way back.

On November 6, a tremendous gale swept over the English fleet. For three days Hawke stood his ground, but he was forced to run back to the shores of England for shelter. Two days later he put to sea again, but the wind was blowing as furiously as ever, and he was again obliged to put back to Torbay. His own ship was rotten and water-logged, so he shifted his flag to the Royal George and struggled out again into the storm.

He was just too late. The French fleet had escaped, and the ships were even now running gaily with the wind behind them down the west coast of France to join the rest of the fleet. Conflans' daring plan might have succeeded had he not had against him a man whose genius, patience, and resolution were proof against the wildest waves and the fiercest winds. In the teeth of the gale Hawke fought his way across the channel to France to find the harbour empty, his prey gone. On ran the French ships before the gale. Very soon the white sails of the English might have been seen hurrying after them. With the waves breaking over their decks, weighed down by the weight of sail, battered by the wild wind that whistled through their rigging, the English ships ran on, every hour bringing them nearer and nearer to the enemy.

"I will attack them in the old way," cried Hawke, "and make downright work of them."

As night drew on, the wind blew harder than ever. Conflans now devised a bold plan. He ran his ships coastwards, among islands and shoals of which he knew the English to be ignorant. It was a wild stretch of dangerous coast, on which the huge Atlantic waves broke with a roar as of thunder, tossing their white foam high into the air. The wind blew with ever-increasing fury, and the night was black as pitch. Only the genius of a Hawke could save the fleet in such a night. But to the successor of Drake and Hawkins all things were possible. "Where there is a passage for the enemy, there, is a passage for me. Where a Frenchman can sail, an Englishman can follow," cried Hawke. "Their pilot shall be our pilot. If they go to pieces on the shoals, they will serve as beacons for us. Their perils shall be our perils."

"And so, on the wild November afternoon, with the great billows that the Bay of Biscay hurls on that stretch of iron-bound coast, Hawke flung himself into the boiling cauldron of rocks and shoals and quicksands. No more daring deed was ever done at sea."

The battle began, and the roar of the guns answered the din of the tempest. The wildly rolling fleets were soon hopelessly mixed up together. Ship after ship went down with its guns and its crews, but the flagship with Hawke on board was making for the white pennant which flew from the mast of Conflans' ship. Soon the two great ships had begun their fierce duel. Night fell before the battle was ended,—a wild night filled with the shrieking of the gale, and morning broke no less wild and stormy. Seven French ships had run for shelter to the coast, two had gone to pieces on the rocks. But in the very centre of the English fleet lay the flagship of Conflans, battered and helpless. In the darkness and confusion of the night the French commander had mistaken his friends for his foes, and anchored unconsciously in the middle of the English fleet.

As the misty grey dawn showed him his mistake, Conflans cut his cables and made for the shore. The battle of Quiberon was over. The French ships were too much damaged to put to sea any more, and Hawke was free to sail home to receive the honours that a joyous England was ready to bestow upon the faithful and brave Admiral who had saved her from a French invasion.

The Boston Tea-ships

"Oh thou, that sendest out the man
To rule by land or sea,
Strong mother of a Lion-line,
Be proud of these strong sons of thine
Who wrench'd their rights from thee."
—TENNYSON.

The year 1759 was a year of victory for England. By the triumph at Plassey Clive had founded the Indian Empire. "With the victory of Wolfe on the Heights of Abraham began the history of the United States;" while Hawke's defeat of the French ships at Quiberon showed the growing strength of the English on the seas.

"We are forced to ask every morning what victory there is," laughed an English statesman, "for fear of missing one."

The year 1762 found peace between England and France, but an unsatisfactory state of things arising beyond the seas in America.

It had cost England very large sums of money to save her colonies from the French. She now demanded those colonies, growing yearly in wealth and prosperity, to help to pay for the war. The colonies were quite willing to do this: they would pay a voluntary sum, but not a sum extracted by means of taxation. England did not understand the spirit of her colonies at this time, and she passed the famous Stamp Act, charging certain stamp-duties in the colonies.

The news that the Stamp Act had actually been passed in England was received in America by a storm of indignation. The colonists denied that the mother country had any right to tax them. Bells were tolled, ships in the harbour flew their flags half-mast high, shops were shut, for it seemed as though the liberty of the American colonies were dead.

Men denounced it openly. "Caesar," cried one in a voice of thunder, "had his Brutus, Charles the First had his Cromwell, and George the Third——"

"Treason! treason!" shouted his hearers.

The young colonist paused.

"George the Third," he finished, "may profit by their example."

A distinguished American, Benjamin Franklin, went to England to protest against the Stamp Act.

"What will be the consequences of this Act?" the English asked him.

"A total loss of the respect and affection the people of America bear to this country, and of all the commerce that depends on that respect and affection," he answered firmly.

"Do you think the people of America would submit to a moderated Stamp Act?" they asked him again.

"No, never!" he cried with emphasis; "never, unless compelled by force of arms."

For the first time in their history the colonies united in the face of a common danger. The colonists held a great Congress. Each colony was represented, and they resolved to resist the Stamp Act.

England was startled by the news: it called Pitt to the front again. He understood the American colonies; he knew the value of their friendship, the danger of their separation. He had been ill when the Stamp Act was passed. Now his old eloquence burst forth again.

"This kingdom has no right to lay a tax on the colonies," he cried. "America is obstinate; America is almost in open rebellion. Sir, I rejoice that America has resisted. Three millions of people so dead to all feelings of liberty as voluntarily to submit to be slaves would have been fit instruments to make slaves of the rest."

His words carried conviction: the Stamp Act was repealed.

In America the news was received with enthusiasm. Bells were rung, bonfires blazed forth, loyal addresses to the King of England were sent across the seas. The quarrel seemed to be at an end.

And the colonies had learnt something of the strength of their union.

The Stamp Act had been repealed, but England reserved the right of regulating American trade by imposing duties upon merchandise imported into the colonies. Discontent again arose; and when, in 1773, a duty on tea was levied, the colonies were ablaze with indignation. They declared that England had no right to enforce a tea-duty, and they refused to receive the tea.

It was the morning of Thursday, December 16, 1773—one of the most momentous days in the history of the world. Seven thousand persons were gathered in the streets of Boston. One of the English tea-ships rode at anchor off Boston harbour and the citizens of the town refused to land the tea unless the duty were repealed. A watch of twenty-five colonists guarded the wharf by day and night, sentinels were placed at the top of the church belfries, post-riders were ready with horses saddled and bridled, beacon fires were prepared on every hill-top, should the English use force to land their tea. There was a law that every ship must land its cargo within twenty days of its arrival.

At sunrise on December 17 the twenty days would have expired. The English ship still lay at anchor with her cargo on board. Would she sail home again, or would her sailors fight?

It was late in the afternoon of the 16th. The crowds waited on into the dusky evening to see what would happen. The old meeting-house was dimly lit with candles, where an important conclave was being held.

"This meeting can do no more to save the country," said a voice amid profound silence.

It was the watchword appointed by the men of Boston to use force. Suddenly a war-whoop was heard through the silent air, and fifty men, disguised as Indians, ran quickly towards the wharf. They were men of standing, wealth, and good repute in the Commonwealth, but in gaudy feathers and paint, with tomahawks, scalping-knives, and pistols. They alarmed the English captains not a little. They quickly cut open the chests of tea on board and emptied the contents of each into the sea. By nine o'clock that evening no less than 342 chests of tea had thus been treated, while the vast crowds of colonists looked down on the strange scene in the clear frosty moonlight.

Next morning the salted tea, driven by wind and wave, lay in long rows along the coast of Massachusetts, while citizens, booted and spurred, were riding post-haste to Philadelphia with the news of Boston's action.

America had at last thrown down the gauntlet for the mother country to pick up.

The great Revolution had begun.

The Declaration of Independence

"Beyond the vast Atlantic tide
Extend your healing influence wide,
Where millions claim your care;
Inspire each just, each filial thought,
And let the natives round be taught
The British oak is there."
—WHITEHEAD (1775).

The hour of the American Revolution had come, but England knew it not. The conduct of the men of Boston roused her wrath, and she prepared punishment. The liberties of Massachusetts—enjoyed for a hundred and fifty years—were taken away: the port of Boston was blockaded.

"The die is cast," said George III. triumphantly. "The colonies must either triumph or submit. We must be resolute."

But there was resolution on the other side of the Atlantic too. A Congress of colonists met at Philadelphia to consider the question. Men from all the thirteen colonies were there, their petty disputes forgotten in the face of this common danger.

"I am not a Virginian, I am an American," said one member, speaking for all.

They now drew up and sent to England their famous Declaration of Rights. They did not ask for independence as yet: they did not want to break with the mother country. They asked for the freedom of their forefathers, for the right of making their own laws and levying their own taxes.

England was astonished and dismayed. Pitt, no longer the Great Commoner but Earl of Chatham, came forward and begged for moderation.

"It will soon be too late," he pleaded. "It is not repealing a piece of parchment that can win back America. You must respect her fears and resentments, and you may then hope for her love and gratitude."

But Chatham's ominous words "availed no more than the whistling of the winds." More English troops were sent out to Boston, and America prepared to resist by force. The call to arms went forth. Washington was made commander-in-chief of the army of the "United Colonies of America." The thunder-cloud so long hanging over the land had broken at last.

Already skirmishes had taken place between the English and Americans, but the first battle was fought at Bunker's Hill in the year 1775. It was one of the strangest battles ever fought. Entrenched on the hills above the town of Boston were some 1600 simple civilian citizens. They had no uniform: each man was dressed in his homely working clothes, each man carried his own gun. All were unskilled in warfare.

At the foot of the hills were 4000 of the finest troops in the world. Their uniforms shone with scarlet, white, and gold, while on their banners blazed the names of famous battles won.

But resplendent as they were, the British troops were unable to endure the destructive fire of the colonists. Again and again they advanced up the hill; again and again they reeled back with shattered ranks, leaving heaps of English dead upon the fire-swept slope.

"Are the Yankees cowards?" shouted the men of Massachusetts, as the English retreated before them.

But there came a time when the colonial troops could hold out no longer. They had fired their last volley, their supply of powder was exhausted, and the English charged the hill and took it.

A hundred and fifteen Americans lay dead across the threshold of their country, but they had shown what they could do.

"How did they behave?" asked Washington anxiously, when he heard news of the battle.

"They stood their ground well," was the proud answer.

"Then the liberties of the country are safe," replied Washington, with a weight of doubt lifted from his heart, as he rode on to take supreme command of the troops.

There was stiff work yet before him. All through the long winter of snow and ice he defended Boston with his raw, ill-fed, ill-armed army, until, in the spring of 1776, the English were obliged to withdraw to New York.

And Washington entered the gates of Boston in triumph, the flag of the thirteen stripes—emblem of the thirteen united colonies—waving above his head.

Gradually an idea of independence was growing in the colonies—of separation from the mother country, who had failed to understand her children. They would have clung to her still, had she but treated them with the consideration they had deserved.

Congress met at Philadelphia, and on July 4 1776 the colonists drew up their famous Declaration of Independence, disclaiming all obedience to the

British crown. The words of the Declaration are still read aloud on the anniversary of every year.

The war was continued with renewed vigour. The sufferings of the Americans were very great, and would have broken the heart of any man of less heroic mould than George Washington. But the autumn of 1777 saw one of his noblest triumphs, when 3500 British soldiers were surrounded and forced to surrender on the heights of Saratoga. It was the turning-point of the war.

"You cannot conquer America," cried Chatham once more. "Redress their grievance and let them dispose of their own money. Mercy can do no harm: it will seat the king where he ought to be—throned in the hearts of his people."

His words were too late. The British disaster at Saratoga had encouraged the French, and early in 1778 France openly allied herself to America, acknowledging the independence of the United States. For five years more the war languished, and then England too had to acknowledge the independence of her colonies. She had learnt a lesson which would teach her in future how much consideration was due to those dependencies which were left.

The United States were now a Republic. Their government was to consist of a President, a Vice-President, and a Congress, to sit at New York.

And who should the colonists choose for their first President but George Washington? He had led them to victory. He should guide them through peace.

As he stepped forward to accept the honoured post a great shout of joy arose from the enthusiastic colonists. He looked an old man now, grown grey and blind in the service of his country. Dressed in simple dark-brown cloth, his sword by his side, he solemnly swore to "preserve, protect, and defend the Constitution of the United States." And so, amid the waving of flags, the ringing of bells, the firing of guns, and the shouts of the people, the great ceremony ended.

George Washington, soldier and patriot, was the first President of the United States of America.

Captain Cook's Story

"We know the merry world is round,
And we may sail for evermore."
—TENNYSON.

While England was struggling with her colonies across the Atlantic, an Englishman, Captain Cook, was sailing away across the Pacific to claim fresh lands for the British crown in New Zealand and Australia. Captain Cook, one of the greatest navigators of his age, had played his part in the American war. To him had been intrusted the difficult task of surveying the intricate channels of the river St Lawrence when Wolfe was making his arrangements to take Quebec from the French.

Born in the year 1728, James Cook had been apprenticed, at the age of thirteen, to a shopkeeper near Whitby, in the north of England. But the life was very distasteful to the boy. Though he knew well enough the roughness of a sailor's life in those days,—of the salt junk they had to eat, of the foul water to drink, of the brutality of the old sea-captain, of disease and death,—yet he longed to go to sea. And one day he tied up his few belongings in his only handkerchief, stole out of the shop at daybreak, passed quietly down the village street, and walked the nine miles to Whitby, where he was taken on board a collier as ship's boy. It was not long before he entered the king's service and went through the Quebec campaign, from which he returned a marked man. He found a keen interest awakening in England with regard to the Pacific Ocean, about which so little was known. Men full of courage had started forth, but limited water, contrary winds, difficulties of getting fresh food, and outbreaks of scurvy, had put an end to each expedition in turn.

Now a new expedition was planned and the command given to Captain Cook. With a crew of ninety-four men, and food for ten months, he sailed from England in a stoutly-built collier, the Endeavour, to explore the Pacific Ocean.

It seems strange to think that at this time Australia and New Zealand were practically unknown in Europe. Not a single white man lived there.

Cook now sailed round Cape Horn, and crossed the Pacific Ocean till he fell in with the east coast of New Zealand, which he found to consist of two islands as large as his own Great Britain. For six months he examined their shores, discovered by Tasman 130 years before. Then leaving the coast at a point he named Cape Farewell, he sailed to the north-west, over a thousand miles of sea, till he touched at last the coast of the great "southern land"—Australia. The country so resembled that which he had left at home that he gave it the name of New South Wales, while to the bay in which they first anchored he gave the name of Botany Bay. The discovery of Botany Bay solved a great problem for England: she was no longer able to send her convicts to Virginia as she had done hitherto, so she sent them to New South Wales instead, and the first settlement of English people in Australia was made at Botany Bay, five miles south of Sydney.

Cook followed the coast of Australia northward for 2000 miles, and after an absence of three years he reached home. But disease and death had overtaken his crew, and the Endeavour was little better than a hospital when she staggered into port at last. Cook had mastered the art of navigation in unknown seas, but he had not solved the problem of how to prevent scurvy killing off his crew after some time at sea.

So, when he was appointed to command the Resolution the following year, with orders to complete the discovery of the southern hemisphere, he gave his whole attention to the subject. This second voyage of Captain Cook marks an epoch in the history of navigation.

He left England with a hundred men on board, and sailed to the Cape of Good Hope, where the Dutch settlement was still prospering. Here he stopped awhile to give his sailors fresh food. "Fresh beef and mutton, new-baked bread, and as much greens as they could eat," he ordered. While at the Cape a Dutch ship came in reporting the death of 150 sailors from scurvy in four months, and Cook took the lesson to heart.

Leaving the Cape he sailed southwards, but a great gale sprang up and blew the ship out of her course, right among some ice-islands of enormous height.

"When we reflected on the danger," said Cook, "our minds were filled with horror. For if our ship ran against the side of one of these islands when the sea was running high, she must have been dashed to pieces in a moment."

Nevertheless he sailed among the ice-islands for many weeks, till he had assured himself there was no land to be found there. The ropes and rigging of the ship were frozen, the decks were sheathed in ice. One bitter morning nine little pigs were born on board the Resolution, but despite every care bestowed on them, they were all frozen to death in a few hours.

At last Cook sailed for New Zealand, for he had now been one hundred days at sea without ever seeing land, while he had sailed 11,000 miles. After so long at sea, under such trying circumstances, it would have been natural to suppose that there must be illness among the sailors. But, thanks to the Captain's precautions, they were all in excellent health.

He now discovered some new islands in the Pacific Ocean, taking possession of them for England—the Friendly Islands, Society Islands, and the Sandwich Islands.

Having completely circumnavigated the globe near the Antarctic circle, Cook returned home with the Resolution. Not only had he left the British flag flying over distant islands in the Pacific Ocean, but he had done what no navigator before him had done,—he had returned, after cruising for three years amid untold dangers, with a clean bill of health. He had lost only one sailor from illness all that time. He had made their health his first care. He had set them an example of eating what was wholesome, however distasteful it might be, and so he had avoided that sailor's scourge—the scurvy.

The account he published of his voyages awoke the interest of Europe in these far-off lands. Englishmen read of coral reefs and palm-trees, of the bread-fruit of Tahiti, the tattooed warriors of New Zealand, of gum-trees and kangaroos, till they felt that this new world of wonders was really their own, and that "a new earth was open in the Pacific for the expansion of the English race."

One last word of Cook himself, by whose steady perseverance and resolution these objects were attained. He was killed in one of the Pacific islands he had discovered; but we like best to think of the stern old sailor, his face set southwards, steering on through the ice-bound seas, thinking not of hunger and cold and monotony, but of how "soon he can break through that wall of ice and learn what is beyond."

James Bruce and the Nile

"In sunset's light, o'er Afric thrown,
A wanderer proudly stood
Beside the well-spring, deep and lone,
Of Egypt's awful flood;
The cradle of that mighty birth,
So long a hidden thing to earth."
—F. HEMANS.

While Captain Cook was exploring the unknown, another man—James Bruce—was opening up the geography of the world in another quarter. There were still many blank spots on the map of the world even in this eighteenth century. For 3000 years the source of the Nile had been a mystery which no man had as yet solved, until it had passed into a proverb that to discover the source of the Nile was to perform the impossible.

This man determined to perform the impossible, and succeeded.

A strong young Scotsman,—athletic, daring, a very giant in height,—James Bruce married the orphan daughter of a wine-merchant in Portugal at the age of twenty-three. She died nine months later, and he travelled off to Spain and Portugal to inspect the vines from which the wine was made. Here he was fascinated by the many Moorish remains, and studied Arabic. He came under the notice of Pitt, and was made consul of Algiers. Before he went, however, Pitt's successor had a talk with the young consul. He alluded casually to the undiscovered sources of the Nile. The idea took hold of Bruce's strong imagination.

"It was at that moment," he says, "that I resolved that this great discovery should either be achieved by me or remain—as it has done for 3000 years—a defiance to all travellers."

For two years he did his duty as consul at Algiers. But the spirit of adventure was strong upon him. He resigned his post and crossed the desert to Tripoli. Here he embarked on board a Greek ship for Crete. A violent storm overtook him, the ship foundered, and Bruce had to swim for his life in the raging sea, to be cast up helpless on the coast of Africa. Lying in an exhausted state on the sands, he was beaten and plundered by Arabs, and after a time sailed once more for Crete and so on to Egypt, where he arrived in the summer of 1768. Having gained the confidence of Ali Bey, the chief of the Mameluke rulers, he obtained leave for his journey to Abyssinia. The country was unruly and wild, cruelty and oppression reigned under the Mameluke rule of those days. It was very different to the Egypt of to-day, where British protection has brought freedom, peace, and prosperity.

Bruce sailed up the Nile, past Thebes, to the first cataract at Assuan. He visited the ruins of Karnak and Luxor, and, crossing the desert on a camel, embarked at a little mud-walled village on the shores of the Red Sea.

After a time he reached Massowah, the port of Abyssinia. The place was little more than a den of thieves and murderers, and had it not been for the kindness of Achmet, the governor's nephew, Bruce would have assuredly been slain. Achmet would fain have detained him altogether. He thought it madness for Bruce to proceed; but the sturdy young Scotsman was true to his trust, and, dressed in the long white Moorish dress of the country, he started for Gondar, the capital.

His way lay across mountainous country, indeed he had to cross the highest mountain in Abyssinia. Food was scarce, hyenas reduced the slender stock of donkeys, storms of rain soaked them to the skin, and often enough the little party were in a sorry plight. Bruce's light clothes were soon in rags, his feet bled from the long tramps over rocky ground, but he pushed bravely on toward Gondar, and at last—ninety-five days after leaving Massowah—he arrived at the capital.

The throne of Abyssinia was still occupied by a supposed descendant of King Solomon; but the country was unsettled and lawless, and many governors strove for the mastery. Smallpox was raging at the palace when Bruce arrived, and he soon showed his skill as a doctor in dealing with the cases. As a reward, the king made him Master of his Horse.

"I told him that this was no kindness. My only wish was to see the country and to find the source of the Nile." But the king would not let him go.

The delay worried the explorer not a little, and at last he persuaded the king to take him on an expedition to the banks of the great river, where there was fighting to be done. For his services the king gave him the district in which the Nile was supposed to rise, and Bruce at last was free to start on this last great quest. Through days of burning heat he pushed on with his local guide. They scrambled over mountains and across scorching plains, until at last Bruce stood on the top of the Abyssinian table-land, and looked down on to the very spot where the springs of the Nile arose. Trampling down the flowers that grew on the mountain-side, and falling down twice in his haste and excitement, Bruce stood at the source of the Nile, gazing at the "hillock of green sod" which has made his name famous.

"It is easier to guess than describe the state of my mind at that moment," he said afterwards, "standing in that spot which had baffled the genius, industry, and inquiry of both ancients and moderns for the course of near 3000 years!"

So far he was right; but after all he had only discovered the source of the Blue Nile in the Abyssinian heights. The White Nile, which joins it at Khartum, was not traced to its source for another hundred years.

It was some time before he could tear himself from the scene of all his hopes and fears to face the hardships of his return journey. Difficult as the outward journey had been, it was as nothing compared to the sufferings and troubles that tried him on the return. It was the autumn of 1772 before he reached Assuan, and eighteen months later before he reached England, after an absence of twelve years. Disappointment awaited him. Not satisfied with the reward of his own success, he expected honours and riches from the country for whom he had risked so much. But people would not believe his wonderful stories. They laughed at the wild tales he told of the Abyssinians, their customs and habits, and Bruce went back to Scotland heart-broken.

Sixteen years later he wrote an account of his travels in five fat volumes, which are among the most interesting in the world of adventure. Long years after his death it was proved that his sayings were true. Anyhow, James Bruce "will always remain the poet, and his work the epic, of African travel."

The Trial of Warren Hastings

"When mercy seasons justice."
—SHAKSPERE.

While Captain Cook was discovering new lands for his country, and America was asserting her independence, events of great importance were taking place in India.

Robert Clive, the victor of Plassey and founder of the Indian Empire, was dead, but the East India Company had found an able successor in Warren Hastings, a man whose name is "writ large across a very important page of Indian history."

Warren Hastings was born in 1732, at a time when the fortunes of his family were at a very low ebb and the old home of his ancestors had passed into strangers' hands. His father was very poor, and little Warren went to the village school. But at the age of seven the boy made a plan. It was to lead him through many glories and many crimes. One bright summer day he lay on the bank of a stream that flowed through the lands of his forefathers, and as he gazed at the old dwelling of his race he swore to himself that some day he would win back his inheritance.

At the age of seventeen he sailed to India as a clerk in the employ of the East India Company. Before long he came under the notice of Clive, who noted him as promising; and he was soon appointed to posts of importance, first at Bengal, then at Calcutta, and later at Madras. In 1771, a few years after Clive's retirement, he was made Governor of Bengal. Here his work was gigantic. He brought order out of chaos; he extended the British Empire in India by his genius, by his patience, by his untiring energy. He enriched the East India Company, and in 1773 he became Governor-General of all the English possessions in India. But his rule henceforth was one of oppression, and misery followed in its train. When he marched against the great Indian warrior, Hyder Ali, who had overrun lands under British sway, he allowed whole native villages to be set on fire, slaughtered the inhabitants, or swept innocent people into captivity.

Here is a story of that injustice which afterwards brought Warren Hastings into such trouble at home. He wanted money not only for himself but for the Company. The Raja of Benares, on the Ganges, was bound to render a certain sum of money to the East India Company every year. The Governor-General now called on him to pay an additional sum, but the Raja delayed. Then Warren Hastings fined him for his delay, and went to Benares to collect the sum himself. With reckless courage he entered the city on the Ganges with a mere handful of men. The Raja still refused to pay the extra fine, and Warren Hastings had him arrested at once and shut in his palace. The palace was guarded by two companies of sepoys or native soldiers, under English officers. But the men of Benares were furious: they killed the Englishmen and slaughtered the sepoys. The Raja then lowered himself to the ground by a rope made of turbans, crossed the Ganges, and made his escape.

Warren Hastings meanwhile was in great peril. He fled for his life, under cover of darkness, from the angry city. Then he sent troops against the mutinous Raja, declared his estates forfeit, and obtained large sums of money, much of which never found its way at all into the treasury of the East India Company.

Rumours of his conduct reached England, and when he returned home in the summer of 1785 he found many of his countrymen boiling with wrathful indignation. There was a statesman named Burke who had a passion for justice. In his eyes the whole career of Warren Hastings in India was stained by a long succession of unjust acts. He had watched the growing empire in India for years with rising wonder and wrath. If England's glory in the East depended on unjust deeds, then he, for his part, would have "refused the gain and shuddered at the glory." With the return of Hastings the time was ripe to strike a severe blow at this system of oppression.

A new spirit of mercy and pity was abroad in England. A sympathy for the sufferings of mankind was moving Englishmen to improve the condition of their jails, to raise hospitals for the sick, to send missionaries to the heathen, and to make crusades against the slave trade. So when Burke made known the conduct of Warren Hastings in India, there was a general outcry throughout the land.

On February 13, 1788, the famous trial that was to last seven years opened in London at Westminster Hall. The great historic place was crowded to overflowing. Its old grey walls were hung with scarlet; the approaches were lined with soldiers; 170 peers attended in robes of scarlet and ermine. The Prince of Wales—afterwards George IV.—was there. All the rank and beauty of England seemed gathered in the great hall on this winter morning.

Warren Hastings entered. He was a small man; his face was pale and worn. He was dressed in a plain poppy-coloured suit of clothes; he bore himself with courage and dignity.

But it was not until Burke, his accuser, rose to speak that the feelings of that great audience were stirred. As England's great orator rose, a scroll of papers in his hand, there was a breathless silence. He began by giving his hearers a vivid picture of Eastern life and customs. Then he accused Warren Hastings of having defied the laws of these Indian people over whom he was ruling in the name of England, of outraging their old customs, destroying their temples, and taking their money by dishonest means. To such a pitch of passion did Burke rise, that every listener in that vast hall, including Warren Hastings himself, held his breath in an agony of horror. So great grew the excitement, that women were carried out fainting, smelling bottles were handed round, while sobs and even screams were heard on every side. The orator ended his famous speech with these words: "Therefore hath it with all confidence been ordered by the Commons of Great Britain that I impeach Warren Hastings of high crimes and misdemeanours; I impeach him in the name of the English nation, whose ancient honour he hath sullied; I impeach him in the name of the people of India, whose rights he hath trodden under foot and whose country he has turned into a desert; lastly, in the name of human nature itself, in the name of both sexes, in the name of every age, in the name of every rank, I impeach the common enemy and oppressor of all."

This was the beginning of the trial: the end was very different. As year after year passed, it still continued. Public interest in it almost ceased as other great events claimed the attention of England. It was not till 1795—seven years afterwards—that the verdict was at last given. Meanwhile public feeling had changed. Pity had arisen for the little Governor-General of India,—the man who had once ruled over fifty millions of people,—as the trial dragged on. And when he was acquitted, there was almost universal applause. Burke had failed to convict the man, but he taught Englishmen that mercy and justice must play their part in the government of the British Empire beyond the seas, and that national honour must go hand in hand with national prosperity.

And Warren Hastings himself? He was a free man now, and he spent the rest of his days at the old home of his forefathers, towards which he had yearned as a little boy, and which he had now won back through much toil and tribulation.

14

Marie Antoinette

"Man is born free, and everywhere he is in chains."
—ROUSSEAU.

These events bring us to the verge of one of the most thrilling and terrible stories in modern history—the great French Revolution.

If the young colonists in America had cried out against unjust taxation, far more grievous was the cry wrung from the peasants of France under a system of taxation that had long existed in their own country. The mass of the people lived and struggled, suffered and died, under painful and cruel conditions. Pitiless indeed were the burdens laid upon the land, until the very life and hope of the nation seemed to be sapped away. The poor were taxed while the rich went free. Duties were laid on articles of daily need—candles, fuel, wine, and grain, while the tax on salt was the hardest of all. Every man, woman, and child over seven years of age had to buy 7 lb. of salt a-year, and a heavy fine was inflicted on those who could not or would not pay. So the nation groaned under its burden. Young women grew old before their time with toil, men worked under a cloud of hopeless gloom, and the nobles of France grew rich and prospered.

Such a state of things could not last. All knew that a change must come sooner or later. Great men—Voltaire and Rousseau—arose and wrote against the existing evils. Voltaire called on the king to take the work in hand. But the years passed on and little was done till, in 1774, the king, Louis XV., died, to be succeeded by his grandson as Louis XVI.

Now four years before this Louis—the Dauphin, as he was called—had married Marie Antoinette, the beautiful young daughter of Maria Theresa, Empress of Germany. The little Marie Antoinette was but fourteen, and the Dauphin fifteen, when a marriage was arranged between them, to cement the peace made a few years since between Austria and France.

Marie Antoinette was the youngest of sixteen children. She was a pretty, careless, pleasure-loving child, captivating all who came near her, and her mother had set her heart on her becoming the Queen of France some day.

It was yet early in the morning of April 21, in the year 1770, when the little Austrian girl left Vienna, her old home, for the long drive to Paris. The streets were thronged, as the long line of carriages rolled through the city gate on their way to the French frontier. A fortnight's driving brought them to Strasburg.

The young German poet Goethe has told us, how here she was met by her new French suite. Her Austrian clothes were taken off, and she was dressed in new clothes from Paris. French ladies, provided for her by the King of France, now came forward to take charge of her. Weeping bitterly, the child kissed her Austrian attendants, sending messages of love back to her mother and sisters at home.

"Pardon me," she said, turning to her French suite and smiling through her tears. "Henceforth I shall never forget that I am French."

On May 16 she was married to the Dauphin, whom she had seen for the first time two days before. A terrific storm burst over Versailles on the wedding-day, causing many a Frenchman to shake his head and prophesy evil.

The young bridegroom himself was but sixteen. He was grandson to the present king. Having lost his father some years before, he was now heir to the throne of France. He had led a solitary life among the splendours and luxuries of the court at Versailles. He was shy and awkward, fond of hunting, but knowing little enough of the pitiable state of that country he would soon be called upon to govern.

Four years after the marriage Louis the king died of smallpox. His grandson and the beautiful young Austrian were King and Queen of France.

"O God! guide us, protect us; we are too young to reign," they cried, falling on their knees with streaming eyes.

For a time it seemed as if brighter days might be dawning for France under the new King Louis XVI. and his minister Turgot, the greatest statesman in France since the days of Richelieu. Turgot tried to make the young king understand how dangerous was the state of his country, how badly in need of reform. He would tax the rich as well as the poor, would abolish forced labour, would give France a national life in which each citizen must bear a part. But Louis was incapable of grasping the great crisis through which his poor country was passing.

"The king is above all, for the good of all," said Turgot.

Louis could not rise to this ideal of kingship, and in 1776 Turgot was dismissed.

"Do not forget, sire, that it was weakness which placed the head of Charles I. on the block," he said at parting. The words were prophetic of what should happen, but his reminder was in vain.

The luxuries at the court now increased. The winter of 1776 was bitterly cold, and bread was very dear. Deep snow lay in the streets of Paris, and the poor suffered acutely.

One day a gay train of sleighs drove through Paris. With every appearance of wealth, comfort, and luxury, Marie Antoinette, the Queen, was enjoying the snow and keen air, with no attempt to hide her merriment. The poor people shivered at their doors. They had never seen sleighs before.

"The Austrian," they muttered with displeasure; for the marriage had never been popular in France, and a feeling grew up between the irresponsible young queen and her unhappy subjects.

It was not till her tragic death seventeen years later, that she atoned for the past by the courage and dignity with which she met her fate.

15

The Fall of the Bastile

"The old order changeth, yielding place to new."
—TENNYSON.

It was in the year 1776 that America made her famous Declaration of Independence. France was the first nation to recognise it, and she sent over men and troops to help the young country in its struggle against oppression. Side by side Frenchmen fought with the English colonists in America. With the settlement they returned to France "with their hearts full of love and their lips loud in praise of the young Republic and its simple splendid citizens."

Among those who fought for France was Lafayette, a friend of George Washington. He now came home to find that the war had cost France more than she could pay, and that something must be done at once, to save the country from hopeless debt.

"Give us the States-General," he cried. "Let the people have a voice in the government of their country."

Soon his cry resounded from one end of France to the other, until the king was obliged to listen. Now the States-General had not met for 175 years. It was a body not unlike the English Parliament, containing members of the Church, the nobles, and the people. Under the last despotic rulers of France, the voice of the people had long been silent. There was danger to the king, when he allowed this great force to be loosened in France.

It was May 5, 1789, when the States-General assembled. The sun shone brilliantly, the streets of Versailles were gay with banners, the air rang with martial music. Eager faces looked down from balcony and window on to the famous pageant. At the head of the procession walked the 600 representatives of the people—a great black-looking mass in their black coats and breeches, black stockings, short silk mantles, and three-cornered hats. Among them walked Mirabeau, with his lion locks of black hair; among them, too, might have been seen the small frail figure of Robespierre—men to play their part in the coming tragedy.

Three hundred nobles followed, in the brilliant dresses of the age—cloaks of gold and high-plumed hats. Among them was Lafayette, the hero of the American war. They were followed by the 300 clergy in "purple and fine linen," and behind all came the King, the Queen, and the Court. Here were plumes and jewels, powdered heads and painted faces, costumes resplendent in the

May sunshine. The whole solemn procession filed into the church of St Louis, and next day the States-General met for business.

A heated discussion on taxation arose. The people proposed that the nobles and clergy should pay taxes as well as themselves. The nobles and clergy refused, and the people formed themselves into a separate body called the National Assembly, and assumed entire control of the State.

Angry days came and went. A cloud hung over the gay Court at Versailles, where the little eight-year-old Dauphin lay dying. But France was too much engrossed with her new life to take much note of the dying child, though he was heir to the French throne. Only Marie Antoinette wept for the drooping of the little royal head, and rained bitter tears on the lifeless body of her eldest son.

Meanwhile the conflict between the king and the National Assembly went on. At last he addressed the whole States-General—nobles, clergy, and people—collected together for the purpose. He would not sanction the National Assembly: they must disperse at once. The king left, the clergy and nobles filed out according to orders. The 600 people sat still.

"Did you hear the orders of the king?" asked one.

"Yes," roared Mirabeau; "and let me inform you, you had better employ force, for we shall only quit our seats at the bayonet's point."

These words were repeated and applauded throughout France. Through the long sultry days of July the storm gathered fast. In Paris it reached its height, and on July 12 it burst.

"To arms! to arms!" shouted one insurgent, and the cry spread like wildfire through the excited city. Military stores were broken open, muskets carried off in triumph, prisons were opened, custom-houses burned. There was none to command, none to obey. Early on the morning of the 14th the fury of the people was directed against the Bastile, the great State fortress and prison of Paris, where for centuries past prisoners had been unjustly thrown. Its double moat and massive walls should have protected it against an unruly mob, but the people were strong and determined in their wrath. Hour after hour, through that long summer day, they fired on the old grey walls, till at last the commander had to surrender.

The Bastile had fallen, and the sun set over a triumphant city of fierce insurgents. Late that night the news reached the king. He was asleep in his palace at Versailles.

"The Bastile has fallen," they told him.

"But," said poor Louis sleepily, "that is a revolt."

"Sire," answered the messenger gravely, "it is not a revolt, it is a revolution!"

The fall of the Bastile was the fall of the old monarchy. The old order passed away on that eventful evening in July. France was shaken to its depths, and the eyes of Europe and America were directed towards the struggling nation.

Three days later, the king made up his mind to go to Paris. While Marie Antoinette wept for his safety he left Versailles. He was pale and anxious. The long highway from Versailles to Paris was "choking with people." Everywhere fluttered the new colours adopted by the people of Paris—red, white, and blue. Everywhere men and even women were armed. In front of him, on a white horse, rode Lafayette. Above them fluttered the tattered banner of the Bastile.

"Long live the Nation!" was shouted on all sides. It was not until Louis reluctantly fixed a cockade of red, white, and blue on his hat that the cry "Long live the King!" was heard.

Meanwhile the National Assembly, now joined by the nobles and clergy, drew up their famous Declaration of the Rights of Man. They swept away all existing orders, declared that all were born equal in rights, that all citizens were equal in the eyes of the law, that virtue and talent entitled a man to office and not birth, that all worship should be free.

The night was far advanced. It was the 4th of August—a marked day in the history of the Revolution.

"But the king, gentlemen," said one who had listened to these sweeping reforms, "the king who has called us after the long lapse of two centuries—shall he not have his reward?"

"Let us proclaim him the restorer of French liberty," they said.

And the Twelve Hundred representatives of the French nation left the blazing hall and made their way home through the warm summer night.

16

The Flight to Varennes

"Before man made us citizens, great Nature made us men."
—LOWELL.

There was now growing a feeling among the people of Paris that the king and the National Assembly should be in their midst, and no longer away at Versailles. So on October 1789, a great mob of citizens, mostly women, set out from Paris to walk to Versailles and bring the king back to his capital.

Lafayette was commander-in-chief of the troops, but it was with a heavy heart that he led the soldiers to Versailles. He felt the Revolution was getting out of all control.

It was a day of rain, and when the mob reached their destination they were weary, hungry, and wet. All through that day and during the night fresh bands of men and women from Paris kept arriving, until early next morning they broke into the palace.

"The king to Paris," shouted the dense throng outside.

Louis stepped on to the balcony and assented to their will.

Then arose a yet more furious cry—

"The queen! the queen!"

Marie Antoinette, with her children clinging to her, now stepped out on to the balcony and looked down on to the sea of furious faces below.

"No children!" was the rough cry.

Pushing them back, the poor queen advanced alone. It was a moment of great peril. Lafayette, afraid for her safety, stepped forward and sought to make her peace with the people. He stooped before them and kissed her hand.

The royal family was then forced to leave Versailles, the palace of Louis XIV. They were never to return. They were taken to a palace in Paris known as the Tuileries,—a cold, deserted dwelling,—where for the next two years they lived the life of captives. The queen spent most of her time with her two children, fearing to venture often beyond the gardens. The king, deprived of his hunting, grew gloomy and ill.

He was powerless in his own kingdom, a mere tool in the hands of the Revolutionists. At last he and the queen resolved to escape from the misery of it all, from a life that had grown almost unbearable. Very quietly they made their plans. The night of Monday, June 20, was fixed for the attempt. Everything was arranged for them by Count Fersen, an intimate friend. In the afternoon the Count paid his last visit to the Tuileries. He had smuggled the last of the clothes for the disguise into the palace. There was a frockcoat and round hat for the king, who was to be a valet; a travelling dress and bonnet for the queen, who was to be governess to her two children; a frock for the little six-year-old dauphin, Marie Antoinette's second son, who was to be dressed as a girl.

Fersen left the queen weeping bitterly, for there was a rumour that the plan had been discovered. The children were put to bed as usual. At nine o'clock supper was served; the queen dismissed her servants and retired to rest. At half-past ten she crept to the little dauphin's room. The child was fast asleep, all unconscious of coming danger. The queen woke him. His sister was already disguised in a cheap muslin dress.

"They dressed my brother as a little girl," she said afterwards, when telling the story of this terrible night. "He looked beautiful, but was so sleepy that he could not stand, and did not know what we were all about."

The queen was dressed as a governess. All was ready. She looked out into the night: everything was quiet. Stealthily the royal fugitives crept through dark unknown passages that warm June night, till they reached the appointed door, which stood unlocked. Then they crossed the courtyard and stepped into the coach, which awaited them with Count Fersen, disguised as a coachman, on the box. Here the king joined them as their valet, and the carriage drove hastily off, through the sleeping streets of Paris.

Outside the city they changed into a new yellow coach, which was to convey them towards the frontier of France. It had been waiting for two hours owing to delays, and the dawn was already breaking in the east.

"Drive—drive as fast as possible," muttered Count Fersen, jumping on to the box beside the German coachman and cracking the whip. "Go faster—faster!"

On they went through the ever-brightening morning, away from the pomps and shams of Paris to the free life beyond the frontier. The king's spirits rose.

"I have escaped from that town of Paris, where I have drunk so much bitterness," he cried joyously.

But he rejoiced too soon: a chapter of accidents now befell the royal family. The horses fell down and broke the harness, which took an hour to mend. They missed a carriage sent to meet them beyond Chalons. But, most fatal of all accidents, the king was recognised by a postmaster named Drouet, who belonged to the Revolution party. The royal party reached Varennes at eleven o'clock that summer night to find they had been discovered.

"If you go a step farther we fire!" cried threatening voices, while guns were levelled at the carriage window. The poor disguised royal family got out. They were led to a grocer's shop hard by and taken up a narrow corkscrew staircase to two small bedrooms. The unhappy queen put her tired children to bed, while the king sat in an arm-chair in the middle of the room in the deepest despair.

In the course of the night a friend of the king arrived and made his way up the narrow staircase to ask for orders.

"I am a prisoner: I have no orders to give," answered Louis in despair.

Even now a little firmness might have saved the situation, and "French history had never come under this Varennes archway to decide itself." But the moment passed. By dawn thousands of peasants had assembled in Varennes. As the sun broke over the lovely valley of the Aire, the grocer begged the king to show himself to the growing crowds in the streets below. Louis obeyed.

"Long live the King! Long live the nation!" cried the people.

"There is no longer a king in France," muttered Louis to his queen, as he read the message from the National Assembly ordering him to return at once.

Slowly and sadly the royal family descended the narrow stairs and entered the carriage once more. Escorted by six thousand guards, they drove back through the glare of a midsummer sun, exposed to the insults of the mob, with blinds up and windows open. The little dauphin slept at intervals, only to awake screaming that he was in a forest where wolves were attacking his mother, the queen.

On Saturday the 25th of June they entered the gloomy palace of the Tuileries again, which they had left so full of life and hope but five days since.

A Reign of Terror

"When France in wrath, her giant limbs upraised,
And with that oath which smote air, earth, and sea,
Stamped her strong foot and said she would be free."
—COLERIDGE.

Guards were now placed inside the palace of the Tuileries as well as outside, sentinels stood in every passage, and the door of each room was kept open day and night. The king and queen dared not venture beyond the gardens for fear of insult and humiliation. From time to time they gave way to outbursts of tears, as they realised the agony of their position.

On June 20, 1792, a mob attacked the Tuileries, burst into the palace, and the royal family barely escaped with their lives.

Meanwhile the Revolution outside was becoming more and more fierce. Mirabeau, the man who might have saved for France her king, was dead. "I carry with me the ruin of a monarchy," he said with prophetic insight as he lay dying.

Lafayette, who had urged moderation, was no longer a power in the land. The country was practically in the hands of three men,—Marat, Danton, and Robespierre,—men whose desire it was, to see the monarchy overturned and a complete Republic established in France.

"Let us depose the king," was their cry.

Gradually Louis was stripped of every emblem of royalty. He was deprived of his sword, his orders of knighthood were taken from him. He was separated from his wife and children. At last he was accused of treason, for having conspired against the will of the people. His trial dragged on amid fierce discussion. When the verdict was given, he was found guilty of treason, and his punishment was death. A last agonised meeting with Marie Antoinette and his weeping children, a passionate entreaty to the little dauphin never to revenge his death, and Louis XVI. of France was led forth to die.

It was a bitter January day in the year 1793 when he was beheaded by the guillotine, a machine erected in a public square in Paris, and used largely during the Revolution.

"Frenchmen, I die innocent," cried the unhappy king to the vast crowds collected to see him die. I pardon my enemies."

"It is done! It is done!" muttered the Frenchmen who had ordained it, rubbing their hands as the crowds dispersed. But as yet they did not realise to the full what they had done. All Europe shuddered with horror at their deed.

"Let us cast down before Europe, as the gauntlet of battle, the head of a king," Danton had cried recklessly.

Austrian and Prussian armies had already collected on the frontiers of France. England, Holland, and Spain now joined in making war on France. Alone stood the stricken nation—alone against the powers of Europe, and rent by quarrels within.

A true Reign of Terror now broke over the whole country. The monarchy had fallen, the Republic was not yet established. The National Assembly, now called the Convention, ruled the country with absolute sway. Violent and ignorant men resolved to blot out all royalists from the country, by means of the guillotine, to accomplish their end. The cry, "Liberty! Equality! Fraternity!" rang from end to end of France. All titles were abolished. Every man and woman, whether noble or shoeblack, was addressed as "Citizen." Numbers left France to take refuge in England and other countries, but numbers were thrown into prison and afterwards guillotined, without even a show of trial. They were carried in carts, with their hands tied behind them, to the place of public execution, often hardly knowing the reason of their death. Peasant girls were beheaded for humming the tune of a royalist song, women for speaking with pity of the victims already perished. All traces of royalty must be swept from the land, cried the tyrants, and swiftly and surely the guillotine did its cruel work. Little children and aged men, ladies of title and women of wealth—all suffered alike. And still the cry rang through the land, "Liberty! Equality! Fraternity!"

At last the queen herself was sentenced. Already the beautiful little dauphin had been torn from her arms, and she had been sent to the common prison. As she passed through the low door she had hit her head. Her attendant had asked if she were hurt.

"No," she answered bitterly; "nothing can hurt me now."

All day long she sat in a kind of stupor, in a dungeon unfit for human use. On October 13, 1793, she was brought forth to her trial. Aged and bent beyond her years, the once beautiful Marie Antoinette stood proudly before her accusers. The trial was short. Three days later, seated in a common cart, her hands bound, she was drawn from prison to the public square where the guillotine stood. There Marie Antoinette, Queen of France, was beheaded. "Oh Liberty! Liberty! How many crimes are committed in thy name!" exclaimed a well-known French lady, Madame Roland, who suffered death on the same spot three weeks later.

One day, when the troubles of the reign of terror were at their height, a young girl, Charlotte Corday, travelled from Normandy to Paris. She had heard of the crimes committed by the leaders of the Convention in the name of Liberty, and she reasoned to herself, if the tyrants could be disposed of, true liberty might be gained for France. She selected Marat for her victim. Going to his house, she obtained an interview with him, and as they talked she drew out a knife and killed him.

"I killed one man," she said, as she faced the death, that her act justly merited—"I killed one man to save a hundred thousand,—to give repose to my country."

Thus fell one of the leaders. The fate of the others was not far distant. Their violence had disgusted even their own party. Both Danton and Robespierre perished by that guillotine to which they had sent so many of their fellow-countrymen.

So the reign of terror ended. At last the object for which so many thousands of lives had been sacrificed was accomplished—France was a Republic. There was no king, there were no nobles. The government was conducted by five Presidents under the name of the Directory.

18

Napoleon Bonaparte

"The childhood shows the man
As morning shows the day."
—MILTON.

But wonderful days were yet in store for this poor storm-tossed France, with the rise of the greatest soldier she has ever known, the greatest conqueror that "ever followed the star of conquest across the war-convulsed earth"—Napoleon Bonaparte. France had but lately annexed the island of Corsica, which lies in the Mediterranean Sea, and had up to this time belonged to Italy. Here, in the year 1769 Napoleon was born. He was but a year old, when Marie Antoinette left her home at Vienna to marry the dauphin of France; he was but seven, when America declared her independence. He was one of nine children—"olive-skinned, black-browed, shrill-tongued" children—a famous family, indeed, where one was to be an emperor, three were to be kings; while of the girls, one was to be a queen and two princesses.

Little enough is known of Napoleon's childhood. His chosen toy was a small brass cannon, his favourite retreat, a solitary summer-house among the rocks by the seaside of Corsica, still known as "Napoleon's Grotto."

One story indeed is told of him in his school-days. The master of the school, where little Napoleon learnt with his elder brother Joseph, arranged a sham fight for his pupils—Romans against Carthaginians. Joseph was ranged on the side of Rome, while his little brother was to be a Carthaginian. But, piqued at being placed on the losing side, the little boy fretted, fumed, and at last stormed, till Joseph offered to change places with him, and he was put on the winning side.

At the age of nine he was sent to a military school in France. Though Joseph wept passionately at the parting, his little brother dropped hardly a tear, though he was deeply attached to his home and his mother.

At school he was proud and silent, holding aloof from his companions, and hating France, because she had taken Corsica from the Italians. He read history eagerly. He delighted in Plutarch's Lives, which told him about the Greek and Roman heroes of old. He loved Cæsar's account of the conquest of Gaul, and spent whole nights pouring over his wonderful exploits. At the age of fifteen he was sent to Paris.

"He will be an excellent seaman," reported his master; "and is worthy to enter the School at Paris."

He was a boy of plain tastes—indeed he had been nicknamed the "Spartan" by his school-fellows—and the luxuries of Paris impressed him deeply. He resented being taught at the expense of Louis XVI., the king who had taken Corsica; but a year later he became lieutenant of artillery, and after eight years' absence returned to his home in Corsica.

His force of character had already made itself felt.

"You, Joseph, are the eldest," said a relation who saw the boys together; "but Napoleon is the head of the family."

His father was dead. He too had cried aloud in his last delirium for his little Napoleon, "whose sword should one day triumph over Europe;" while Rousseau had prophesied of Corsica, "This little island will one day be the astonishment of Europe."

August 10, 1793, found him in Paris at the storming of the Tuileries by the Revolution mob, when the king and queen with difficulty escaped.

"If Louis XVI. had mounted his horse the victory would have been his," Napoleon had cried with disdain.

The next two years were spent between Corsica and France. He tried many things, and failed in all. He was nearly twenty-five, and wholly unknown, when his chance came to him. Full of unbounded ambition, he was ready to act wherever glory was to be found. He might have thrown in his lot with England or with Italy. He threw it in with the Republicans of France. Louis had been beheaded, and the reign of terror was at its height. The Republic was carrying on war with the Royalists without pause, without mercy.

Toulon was the great southern military storehouse of France, and Toulon had declared for the Royalists. Not only this, but they had proclaimed as King, Louis XVII., the poor little eight-year-old dauphin, now languishing, fatherless and motherless, in a Paris prison. The English were helping the men of Toulon to hold the town, and to guard the hilly frontage of fifteen miles, which commanded the sea. Napoleon, now serving the Republic, arrived at Toulon in September, and at once took command of the artillery. Everything was in confusion, but he saw clearly what alone would give him the Royalist city. The French must sweep the harbour with their fire, force the British ships to retire, and Toulon must fall into the hands of the Republic.

It was the night of December 17, 1793. Torrents of rain were falling, a wild wind raged over the Mediterranean Sea, while flashes of lightning added new terrors to the night. In the midst of this Napoleon made a determined attack on the British defences, which were soon swept by his guns. So deadly was the fire, there was nothing left the Royalists but surrender. A terrible scene followed. A magnificent French fleet lay in the harbour at Toulon. Desperately the Royalists turned on it. They set fire to a powder-ship, and soon the flames of the burning ships lit up the surrounding country. Prisoners broke loose from the town, and by hundreds and thousands, the inhabitants of Toulon flocked to the beach, begging for means of escape from the Republicans. Above the howling wind arose their pitiful cries for mercy. Napoleon never forgot the terrors of that night. "The whirlwind of flames and smoke from the arsenal resembled the eruption of a volcano, and the vessels blazing in the roads were like so many displays of fireworks. The masts and forms of the vessels were distinctly traced out by the flames, which lasted many hours, and presented an unparalleled spectacle." So he wrote long years after, during his imprisonment at Helena.

Thus Napoleon Bonaparte sprang into fame. From this time onwards he advanced by rapid strides to that greatness which has given him such a conspicuous place in the history of the world.

19

Horatio Nelson

"Thine island loves thee well, thou famous man,
The greatest sailor since our world began."
—TENNYSON.

Among the ships that had sailed into the harbour of Toulon under the flag of Admiral Hood was the Agamemnon, under the command of Horatio Nelson. He was not present on that fateful night when the British fleet had to escape into the storm, as he had been sent to Naples with despatches. But it is strange to think that the two greatest figures in the war between England and France should "for a moment have crossed each other's path at this very beginning of the struggle."

Nelson was born in Norfolk, England, eleven years before his great enemy Napoleon. Like the little Napoleon, he was one of a large family. His mother died when he was but nine years old. At an early age he was sent to school, and of his school-days many stories have been told. Here is one.

The brothers William and Horatio Nelson were returning to school on their ponies, after the Christmas holidays. The snow lay deep, and the boys thought this a good enough excuse for turning home again.

"The snow is too deep to venture farther," said William, as he met his father in the hall.

"If that indeed be the case, you shall certainly not go," was the reply; "but make another attempt, and I will leave it to your honour. If the road be found dangerous, you may return; yet remember, boys, I will leave it to your honour."

Off they set again. The road now became almost impassable with drifts of snow, but although the danger was great Horatio refused to return.

"We have no excuse," he said firmly. "Remember, brother, it was left to our honour."

Horatio Nelson was twelve years old when, one day, he heard that his uncle had been made captain of a large ship. The boy knew that his father was very poor, and had a struggle to bring up his eight motherless children. So he begged that his uncle might be asked to take him to sea. He was a sickly and fragile-looking little boy, and his uncle's answer was not exactly encouraging.

"What has poor little Horatio done," he cried, "that he, being so weak, should be sent to rough it at sea? But let him come; and if a cannonball takes off his head, he will at least be provided for."

Sad enough is the first picture of the little would-be sailor. It was a dull grey morning when he arrived at Chatham, and the boy shivered with cold as he wandered about the dockyard looking for his uncle's ship, bewildered by the strange sights that met his eyes for the first time.

After all his uncle's ship did not sail, and the boy was put on board a ship bound for the West Indies. At first he was very unhappy, and as he paced the broad quarter-deck of the vessel, ploughing her way over the stormy waters of the North Atlantic Ocean, he yearned after his distant home in England. The voyage suited him well, and he returned, in 1771, a sunburnt lad of thirteen, with "every hair a rope-yarn and every finger a fish-hook."

He now joined a ship bound for the North Pole, and amid the frozen silence of the far north he learnt some of the lessons of his life.

One night,—so runs one story of him,—young Nelson and another youth stole away from the ship, which was fast among the ice, to try their luck in shooting a bear. Nelson, armed with a rusty musket, led the way in high spirits over frightful chasms of ice. It was not long before the two young adventurers were missed. A thick fog had come on, and the captain of the ship was in great anxiety about the boys. Between three and four in the morning the fog lifted, and the boys were discovered at some distance attacking a large bear. A signal was made to them to return at once. Nelson's companion obeyed.

"Let me but get one blow at him," cried Nelson eagerly.

But the captain saw what peril the boy was in. He fired hastily, and frightened the bear away. When Nelson returned he was severely scolded for his conduct, though the captain could not but admire the fearless courage of the young midshipman. Nelson was greatly agitated. "Sir, I wished to kill the bear, that I might carry its skin to my father," he murmured in self-defence.

At the age of fifteen Nelson possessed all the knowledge of an able seaman. In 1773, when Napoleon was but four years old, he was sailing off to the East Indies. But here the climate told on him. Disease took hold of him, he was wasted to a mere shadow, and sent home. Bitterly disappointed at the seeming failure, he felt he would never rise in his chosen profession. He fretted miserably about it, till one day he took himself in hand. "I will be a hero," he cried, "and, confiding in God, I will brave every danger."

This resolve to "do" now became the watchword of his life. It was an ever-growing passion till it ended in the grand finale, which will ring down the ages—"England expects every man to do his duty."

Nelson was appointed to the Agamemnon in 1793, and a few days later the French Republic, then at its fiercest heat, declared war on Great Britain and Holland. The dawn of a great war stirred the blood of English boys, and Nelson received a number of young midshipmen on board. Among them was Josiah Nisbet, his stepson, a boy about thirteen years old at this time. To these young sailors he gave this advice: "First, you must always implicitly obey orders, without attempting to form any opinion of your own respecting their propriety; secondly, you must consider every man as your enemy who speaks evil of your king; and thirdly, you must hate a Frenchman as you do the devil."

So in the year 1793 we have these two men—Nelson, a rising sailor in the service of England; Napoleon, a rising soldier in the service of the French Republic.

While they are preparing for the great struggle that was soon to take place, let us turn to two great explorers who were now playing their parts in unfolding the geography of Africa and South America.

20

The Adventures of Mungo Park

"Strong in will
To strive, to seek, to find, and not to yield."
—TENNYSON.

When the young Scottish surgeon, Mungo Park, started forth on his travels, to find out about the mysterious river Niger, little was known of the interior of Africa. It was twenty-six years since Bruce had discovered the source of the Nile, and still men thought that the Niger rose near it and flowed right across the Dark Continent from east to west, its mouths being the rivers Senegal and Gambia on the west coast. It had long been the dream of men of all nations to reach not only the Niger, but also the wonderful city on its banks called Timbuktu, which was said to be paved with gold.

In the year 1795, when the French Revolution was still at its height, Mungo Park, a young man of twenty-four, offered his services to the British African Society to explore this region. Tall and strong, with an iron will and a sweet expression, was this Mungo Park. He had already been to the East Indies, and a thirst for travel and adventure had seized him. He arrived on board an African trading-vessel, in May 1795, at the mouth of the Gambia, and sailed thence up the river to the English depot at Pisania. Here he was touched by the wretched condition of the slaves, who were brought from the interior and shipped to England to supply the European market. But his work lay in another direction.

It was December before he was ready to start. His sole companions were a negro servant and a slave boy. He took a horse for himself and two donkeys for his servants, food for two days, some beads and tobacco for exchange, a few clothes, an umbrella, compasses, a thermometer, besides a couple of pistols and a few firearms.

Thus provided, thus attended, thus armed, Mungo Park started for the heart of Africa. It must have needed a stout courage indeed, plenty of young enthusiasm and confidence, to face the unknown thus scantily equipped. Waterless deserts, trackless jungles, gloomy forests, angry natives—all had to be encountered before the Niger could be reached.

It is not possible to follow him in detail, interesting as his travels are. Now we see him standing before some black king begging leave, by means of gifts, to pass through his dangerous country. Now he is stealing forth silently under the moonlit sky to escape from furious natives, to pass the night in some great forest, where wild beasts made the night hideous with their howls. Now he is passing through country of untold beauty, where the windings of the Senegal, descending from its rocky heights, lend a pleasing variety to the scene. The banks of the Senegal were reached two days after Christmas. The next part of the road lay through an inhospitable region, inhabited by negroes of the most degraded type. So threatening were they, so brutal in their conduct, that the two native servants refused to venture farther, and Mungo Park went forward alone. Gathering together the few possessions now left him, he stole away under cover of the darkness, and with a stern resolution, unsurpassed in history, started on his forlorn hope of reaching the mysterious Niger. From all sides came the roar of wild beasts, adding terror to his already dangerous situation. But undismayed he plodded on, alone, through the night.

Suddenly one day he was seized and dragged before a black Moorish king, and all hope seemed to fade away. Men, women, and children crowded round to see the white man. He was insulted, tortured, starved. Day after day passed, leaving him no means of escape. The desert winds scorched him, sand-storms choked him; the heavens above were like brass, the earth beneath as the floor of an oven. Fever came on him, and he feared death with his great work yet unfinished. It was the end of May before he escaped from this intolerable life.

Early one morning, when the sun was just breaking across the sky and the Moors round him were sleeping heavily, he took his bundle, stepped stealthily over the sleeping negroes, jumped on to his horse, and rode away as fast as possible. But the horse, like its master, was reduced to mere skin and bone after four months' captivity. Every moment was one of life or death. Once he looked round to see three Moors on horseback in full pursuit. They were brandishing weapons and screaming threats, but he escaped, and rode breathlessly forward. Starvation now stared him in the face. To the pangs of hunger were added the agony of thirst. There was no water. The sun beat pitilessly down, the sand reflected the heat as from a furnace. Night came. His horse grew too tired to carry him any longer, but with his old strength of will he staggered on in the darkness, often falling from very weakness. Suddenly a flash of lightning bespoke a coming storm. On his ear fell the welcome sound of trees bending before a wind. It put new life into the fever-stricken explorer. But a terrific sand-storm swept over the land, and he fell down hopelessly under a sheltering bush. Then followed great storm-clouds, and soon big drops of rain began to fall, while lightning flashed and thunder crashed above. The refreshing rain fell on to his burning face and shaking hands, and saved his life.

In the third week of his flight his reward came. The prize for which men and nations had struggled for three centuries was to be his. Let him tell his own story. "Looking forward," he says, "I saw with infinite pleasure the great object of my mission—the long-sought-for, majestic Niger, glittering in the morning sun, as broad as the Thames at Westminster and flowing to the east-ward. I hastened to the brink, and having drunk of the water, lifted up my fervent thanks to the great Ruler of all things for having thus far crowned my endeavours with success."

He was the first European to reach the Niger, and to tell the world that its course was "towards the rising sun," and not as men had thought.

But his troubles were not ended here. The natives would not allow him to enter their city Sego on the Niger, and he wandered away to take shelter from the sun under a tree. Hour after hour passed away and no one offered him food or lodging. The sun fell and a great storm gathered. Suddenly a poor negro woman passed him returning from her work. Seeing his pitiful condition she stopped to ask his story. Bidding him follow her, she took him in, broiled him a fish from the river, and spread a mat for him to sleep upon. And while he slept she sang with her companions of this strange new guest:—

"The winds roared and the rains fell,
The poor white man sat under our tree;
He has no mother to bring him milk,
No wife to grind his corn."

Far on into the night the women of Africa sang, as they worked—

"Let us pity the white man, no mother has he."

Mungo Park could not get much farther. Fever had reduced him to a mere skeleton, his one remaining shirt was threadbare. He made his way slowly back to the coast and thence to England, where he arrived after an absence of two years and nine months.

As the years passed on he longed to be back in Africa. He felt much remained to be done, and the early part of the new year 1805, found him leaving England for the last time. It was May before he left Pisania, this time with forty-four Europeans and a large quantity of baggage. It was August before he caught sight of the Niger, by which time most of his companions were either dead or dying. But his stout heart did not despair as he embarked on his last great venture, "with fixed resolution to discover the source of the Niger or perish in the attempt."

In a large, unwieldy, half-rotten canoe—christened His Majesty's schooner Joliba—he set sail with nine men to navigate the strange new river, studded with dangerous rocks, full of hippopotamus, whose banks were lined with cannibal tribes. This is the last sight we get of Mungo Park, gliding down the Niger towards the heart of savage Africa, into the deep darkness of the unknown. The rest is silence.

Years after, it was discovered that he had sailed some thousand miles down the river, past Timbuktu to Boussa. Here the boat was overturned by rapids, and, at the last, attacked by natives. The great Niger had claimed the brave explorer as her own.

The Travels of Baron Humboldt

"I am going, O my people,
On a long and distant journey;
Many moons and many winters
Will have come and will have vanished,
Ere I come again to see you."
—LONGFELLOW.

While Mungo Park was making his way into the heart of Africa, another man was turning his thoughts towards South America, the geography of which was still very uncertain.

Baron Humboldt, whose discoveries were to enrich the world, was born in 1769—the same year as Napoleon and Wellington—at Berlin, where his father occupied a high position at the Court of the King of Prussia. As a little boy, Humboldt was taught by the man who had translated Robinson Crusoe into German, and his mind was soon filled with the spirit of adventure from reading the new story-book. But even the feats of Robinson Crusoe grew small beside those of the boy's next friend—Forster. Forster had not been wrecked on a desert island, but he had actually sailed round the world with Captain Cook, and had written an account of his adventures. His desire to travel grew more and more intense as the years passed on. His mind turned towards South America.

He read the chronicles of Balboa and Pizarro. and the grand old Spaniards of the sixteenth century. He learnt mining and geology, then a new science. He talked of his plans to Goethe and Schiller, the world-famed poets. He went to Paris to make known his great desire, and then, leaving home and luxury and a life made pleasant by many friends, he started for the unknown.

The spring of 1799 found him at Madrid, seeking leave from the King of Spain to visit the Spanish dominions in America. For at this time the main part of South America still belonged to Spain by reason of her conquests. The names of Columbus, Vespucci, Cabral, Balboa, Pizarro, Raleigh,—all rise before us in turn when we speak of South American discovery, while in North America, Cortes had gained Mexico for Spain.

Early in June 1799 Humboldt set sail from Corunna on board the Pizarro. He was accompanied by a young Frenchman, Bonpland, a man of science and a congenial companion. Slowly the coast of Europe faded from sight. They would not see it again for five years. Twelve days' sailing brought them to the Canary Islands, where they landed for Humboldt to go up the Peak of Tenerife, a volcano which had recently been very active. They sailed on over the southern seas, deeply impressed with the beauty of the southern skies. As they neared the equator, star after star they had known from childhood sank lower and lower, until apparently lost in the sea. The whole heaven seemed to change, until they hailed with delight the Southern Cross, or the four stars that form, roughly, a cross in the southern hemisphere.

Forty-one days after leaving Corunna they saw the coast of South America, and landed at Cumana, on the north coast of Venezuela. It was their first sight of the tropics. The deep silence, the brilliant colours, the gigantic trees, the strange birds, all impressed them deeply. Humboldt wrote down all his observations, and when he reached home again he gave them to the world, which was soon ringing with his fame. He studied everything: the stars in the heavens, the earthquakes which shook the earth; flowers, animals, shells, trees, the weather and temperature. His eyes and ears were ever open to take in all that Nature could tell him of her great and mysterious secrets. He rejoiced in the beautiful plains and valleys of Venezuela, watered by the vast Orinoco, and soon started off on an expedition into the very heart of things. In a large native canoe he sailed up the river with his friend. In a cabin made of palm-leaves, a table was made for him of ox-hides strained over a frame of Brazil-wood at one end of the boat, where he could sit and write. Many were the stories he told on his return. It was a voyage of peril and wild adventure for the two white men making their way into unknown regions. Never had they seen nature so wild and grand. Gigantic trees and tropical forests, grassy plains and vast rolling rivers abounded.

"The crocodile and boa rule the rivers; the jackal and other wild beasts rove here without fear or danger through the forests," says Humboldt.

Often he found immense tracts of country uninhabited by any human beings. Once he came upon a tribe of natives who made a practice of fattening and eating their wives. One of the deepest impressions was made by the huge cataracts on the Orinoco, at which he and Bonpland stood and gazed in awe. Never before had they seen such masses of foaming waters or such colossal black rocks rising from their surface.

After a journey of seventy-five days, during which they travelled no less than 375 miles, they returned to Guiana. They had sailed on five great rivers, they had discovered the union of the Orinoco and Amazon, the largest river in the world, and they made new maps of this hitherto unexplored region.

It is impossible to follow their wanderings, but their ascent of Chimborazo is interesting. At the time it was supposed to be the highest mountain in the world, but it was scaled by an Englishman, Whymper, in 1880, and it is now known that Mount Everest in the Himalayas is much higher.

January 1802 found the travellers at Quito, one of the most charming cities in South America. It stands among gigantic mountains and almost under the shadow of Cotopaxi, the highest volcano in the world. It is the capital of Ecuador (Equator). Humboldt, with two friends—a Frenchman and a Spaniard—arrived one fine day at the foot of Chimborazo, and they began the ascent on mules. They went steadily upwards till they reached a lake, which was already higher than the highest mountain in the Alps. Already they had attained the highest spot yet reached by human foot. The mules could go no farther, so the travellers went on foot. Over fields of newly-fallen snow, they gained a narrow ridge which led to the top. The path grew very steep and slippery, and their guides refused to go farther. Nothing daunted, the travellers went on. A thick mist now surrounded them. Their path was but ten inches broad. On one side was a chasm a thousand feet deep, on the other was a steep slope of snow covered with a glassy coat of ice. One false step meant certain death. Soon they had to crawl on hands and knees, but their courage was high, and they went doggedly on.

The fog grew thicker: they suffered from the rarity of the air. Breathing was difficult, and mountain sickness came on. Their heads swam, their lips bled, their eyes grew bloodshot. Suddenly the fog lifted, and they saw the summit. They hurried forward, filled with a great hope, when right across the ridge they saw a huge chasm which it was impossible to cross. By this time they were nearly frozen with cold. A great snowstorm broke over the top, and they were forced to turn back without having reached the summit. But they had reached a height of 19,200 feet above the sea, an altitude since surpassed, but never attained by man till that June day in 1802 by Humboldt and his two faithful friends.

It would take too long to tell how they crossed the lofty chain of the Andes and explored Peru, how they reached Lima, with its beautiful cathedral where Pizarro, its founder, lies buried; how they sailed north to Mexico, and finally, after an absence of five years, returned safely to Europe.

He went many another journey after this, and earned for himself the name of the "Monarch of Science," the "Father of Physical Geography." He outlived his contemporaries Napoleon and Wellington by many long years. Long after the "Great Captain" had done his wars and the "Great Despot" had suffered for his ambition, the "Monarch of Science" was winning his victories in a quiet way that cost no tears to others, but enlarged the boundaries of the world of thought beyond all human ken.

The Beginning of the Struggle

"Admirals all for England's sake,
Honour be yours; and fame
And honour, as long as waves shall break,
To Nelson's peerless name."
—H. NEWBOLT.

Let us turn again to Napoleon and Nelson, now ready to begin their conflict.

It has been said that nothing in the history of the world is quite so wonderful as the history of Napoleon, with its monstrous triumphs and its tragic fall,—nothing is more wonderful than the history of France immediately after the Revolution. Her success in the wars that followed was immense, until, in the year 1796, she had won over as her friends Spain and Holland, though England and Austria were still her enemies. Now Austria ruled over a great part of Northern Italy, and it was against her that Napoleon was first sent in the spring of this year.

"Soldiers, you are half starved and half naked," said the young commander to his troops. "I will lead you into the most fertile valleys of the world: there you will find glory and riches."

His success in North Italy astonished not only France but Europe. The "Little Corporal," as his soldiers called him, fought eighteen pitched battles and won them all, till in little over a year he had made himself master of Italy and changed the face of Europe. He returned to Paris amid boundless enthusiasm. He had conquered the Austrians, but the English were still formidable.

"Go!" cried one of the Directors of France, clasping Napoleon to him,—"Go, capture the giant corsair that infests the seas."

Let us turn for a moment to the "giant corsair," and understand the danger of its strength to France. This very year the English had gained two great naval victories over the allies of France—Spain and Holland.

The first was fought off Cape St Vincent, where a Spanish fleet of twenty-seven ships was waiting to join two French fleets, when 100 sail would sweep proudly over the seas to invade the British Isles. Sir John Jervis, the English admiral, was cruising off Cape St Vincent, a headland on the coast of Portugal, to prevent the union of the fleets. Nelson was in command of one of his ships—the Captain. "The fate of England hung on the part he was about to play."

It was but daybreak on the morning of February 4, when a hazy dawn suddenly lifted, disclosing to the English admiral the Spanish fleet not far away. Huge ships loomed large out of the fog. Jervis signalled to prepare for battle.

"There are eight ships, Sir John," they reported to him, as one by one they appeared.

"There are twenty ships, Sir John," they reported presently.

"Very well," was the undaunted answer.

"There are twenty-seven ships, Sir John," was the next report, "and we are but fifteen."

"Enough—no more of that. The die is cast, and if there were fifty sail I would go through them."

The battle soon began. It would take too long to tell how Nelson was the moving spirit of it all,—how, with the genius of a great commander, he alone read the purpose of the Spanish admiral, and how he took the one step that saved England.

"Victory or Westminster Abbey!" he had cried, as with fiery zeal he had climbed the bulwarks of a huge Spanish vessel.

So the Spaniards were beaten, and the proposed invasion of Great Britain did not come off this time.

But there was danger of invasion from another of those allies who had recently made their peace with France. The Dutch navy was still renowned: it would help France to defeat England on the high seas.

All through the spring of this year—1797—a splendid Dutch fleet had been lying in the Texel, ready to take French troops to the invasion of Great Britain.

For five long months Admiral Duncan, of the British fleet, had blockaded the enemy's ships at the mouth of the Texel. But mutiny broke out amid English sailors, and one day nearly all his ships spread their sails and disappeared away to England to join the other mutineers. Admiral Duncan now did one of the pluckiest deeds ever chronicled in the annals of the sea.

"Keep the Texel closed!"—these were his orders. He would not fail in obedience. He knew there were some ninety-five ships in the Texel, thirty-three being battleships. Mustering his crew, he told the men that he meant to do his duty till the ship sank. They were in shallow water, and even when they were at the bottom, the flag of England would still fly above them.

" 'I've taken the depth to a fathom!' he cried,
'And I'll sink with a right good will;

For I know when we're all of us under the tide
My flag will be fluttering still.'"

So he anchored his ship at the mouth of the Texel, where the channel was very narrow, and there for three days and nights he "corked up the bottle which held the Dutch fleet." It was a moment of peril—one of the gravest perils of the whole war—when stout-hearted Admiral Duncan represented the sea power of England. In order to deceive the Dutch captains, he kept gallantly signalling to an imaginary fleet beyond the sky-line. The long hours of loneliness and anxiety passed, and the Dutchmen, cooped up in the river mouth, little dreamt that they were being held in check by a "deserted admiral upon a desolate sea."

When at last the Dutch ships emerged, Duncan's danger was over. His faithless vessels had returned to him, and he was only waiting his chance to fight the fleet of Holland. The two fleets met at last off the coast, on the morning of October 11. It was a squally day, and the ships rolled heavily in the dark waters of the North Sea, where the English and Dutch fleets strove for the mastery. The Dutch fleet was one of the finest that ever put to sea, and the men fought with a stubborn courage worthy of their old fame. It was not till their ships were riddled with shot, their masts falling, and their sailors dying by hundreds, that the Dutch admiral, De Winter, was obliged to surrender to the English. The victory assured, old Admiral Duncan—for he was sixty-six—called his crew on deck, and with faces still black with powder, they knelt on the "shot-torn planks" to thank God for their success.

So the crushing victory of Camperdown consoled "one of the bravest of the brave for an agony unrivalled in the story of the sea."

Admiral Duncan had broken the naval strength of Holland. No more need England fear her power by sea.

22

The Battle of the Nile

"O saviour of the silver-coasted isle!
O shaker of the Baltic and the Nile!"
—TENNYSON.

"Let us destroy England!" exclaimed Napoleon impatiently; "that done, Europe is at our feet."

It was evident, after the victories of Cape St Vincent and Camperdown, that England was too strong to be encountered by sea again. But Napoleon had gigantic schemes of his own. He would attack England in distant India, he would restore to France the great kingdom of the East. English troops were now in possession of the Cape of Good Hope, therefore Napoleon planned the route through Egypt to India. The shadowy East appealed to the strong imagination of the young Corsican soldier.

"Europe is but a molehill," he said; "all the great glories have come from Asia."

Very quietly he now set to work preparing for his conquest of Egypt. England must know nothing of it. In the summer of 1798 all was ready, and one May morning, the sun rose on the white sails of the French transports, as they left Toulon.

"In the name of Liberty I am come to lead you across mighty seas and into remote regions, where your valour may win such glory and such wealth as can never be looked for beneath the cold heavens of the west," said Napoleon to his soldiers at starting. No expedition so vast and formidable in strength had ever set sail from the French coast before as that, which now swept proudly down the Mediterranean Sea, while England guarded her own coasts for the invasion that never came.

The French fleet having captured Malta, arrived off Alexandria on July 1, and the troops disembarked in a violent gale, their boats being nearly swamped by the surf.

Alexandria fell without a struggle, and the army set out for the long desert march to Cairo.

On the 21st Napoleon and his army came within sight of the Pyramids, and found the enemy drawn up to receive him.

"Soldiers," he cried, "forty centuries look down upon you from the top of yonder pyramids."

The battle of the Pyramids was fought and won, and the victorious French started back for the coast.

Meanwhile it became known to England that the French fleet was in the Mediterranean Sea, and Nelson with an English fleet was despatched at once in quest. After searching for some time, he arrived off Alexandria on August 1 to find the long-sought fleet riding at anchor in Aboukir Bay, some fifteen miles from Alexandria; and the look-out from the mast-head of the admiral's flagship beheld the gleam of white sails in the afternoon sunshine with feelings akin to despair. The afternoon wore on, and the French ships lay motionless on the smooth waters of Aboukir Bay. None thought that Nelson would dare attack them till morning. But they did not know the English admiral.

"Fear? I never saw fear. What is it?" he had asked, when little more than a baby. He did not know at the age of forty. He made up his mind to attack at once. It was his first command, and his first magnificent chance.

"If we succeed, what will the world say?" said one of his captains.

"There is no if in the case," replied Nelson; "that we shall succeed is certain. Who may live to tell the story is another question."

Nelson had already lost one eye and his right arm in battle, but he was undaunted. The order to advance was given, and soon the gleaming sails of the English ships were scudding over the afternoon waters of the Mediterranean. They entered Aboukir Bay in grim silence. One by one the battle-ships took up their positions between the French ships and the coast, in such a way that two English ships attacked one French; and at half-past six, as the sun was setting in the west, the battle began. By seven o'clock black darkness had fallen over land and sea; but the flashing lights filled the heavens, and the booming guns broke the silence of the eastern night.

Early in the night Nelson was badly wounded in the forehead—so badly that he cried, "I am killed." They carried him below. The surgeon was attending a poor sailor, who had been badly wounded. When he saw Nelson being carried down, apparently dying, he left the sailor and hurried to the side of the admiral.

"No," murmured Nelson in his agony; "I will take my turn with my brave fellows."

Suddenly, in the middle of that savage night of battle, the French flagship exploded. Flames in great sheets shot up into the moonless sky, as from a volcano. The water hissed, as blazing masses of rigging and timber shot up only to fall into the troubled bay. The French Admiral perished, and a hush fell on every man in the two fleets. No gun was fired, for all seemed paralysed with the awful sight of that burning ship. Among those who perished in the flagship was the ten-year-old Casabianca, who refused to leave his post without his father's leave, and that father was already dead below.

> "The boy stood on the burning deck
> Whence all but he had fled;
> The flame that lit the battle's wreck
> Shone round him o'er the dead."

Morning dawned to find two French ships alone unconquered, and these saved themselves by flight. Thus ended the battle of the Nile, one of the most important naval battles ever fought. For it put an end for the present to the naval power of France, and it gave to England absolute command of the Mediterranean.

The news reached Napoleon on his desert march.

"To France," he said with a sigh, "the Fates have decreed the empire of the land; to England the empire of the sea."

"We have no longer a fleet," he said later. "We must either remain in this country, or quit it as great as the ancients."

23

Copenhagen

"Of Nelson and the North
Sing the glorious day's renown,
When to battle fierce came forth
All the might of Denmark's crown."
—CAMPBELL.

The news of Nelson's great victory spread over Europe rapidly. The Italians were specially pleased at Napoleon's defeat, since he had overrun their country.

"Oh, brave Nelson!" cried the Queen of Naples, a sister of Marie Antoinette, bursting into tears. "God bless and protect our brave leader. Oh Nelson, Nelson, what do we not owe you,—Victor, saviour of Italy!"

England's navy had grown very formidable. She had within a short time defeated the Spanish fleet off Cape St Vincent, the Dutch fleet off Camperdown, and the French fleet off the coast of Africa. Three fleets had been destroyed, but the great northern fleet yet remained. There was the fleet of Russia, begun by Peter the Great a hundred years before, the fleet of Sweden, and the fleet of Denmark. And these three northern powers now united, to destroy the growing strength of England's sea power.

Brilliant leader though he was, Nelson was only second in command on this expedition against the northern fleets. His chief was Sir Hyde Parker, a man who finally intrusted the command practically to the hero of the Nile.

Nelson joined the fleet at Yarmouth in Norfolk, England, in the autumn of 1800. He found the admiral nervous at the prospect of "dark nights and fields of ice."

"I hope," said Nelson, "we shall give our northern enemies that hailstorm of bullets, which gives our dear country the dominion of the seas. We have it; and all the devils of the north cannot take it from us if our wooden walls have fair play."

So eighteen great battleships fought their way across the stormy North Sea to Denmark. Their orders were to negotiate, if possible, rather than fight; so when they arrived at the northern point of Denmark, known as the Skaw, they anchored, and a messenger was sent forward to negotiate under a flag of truce. The delay irritated Nelson sorely.

"I hate your pen-and-ink men," he said; "a fleet of British warships are the best negotiators in Europe. While negotiations are going on, the Dane should see our flag waving every time he lifts his head."

But the eighteen battleships, with their tall masts and huge wooden hulls, stood without the Sound, and the northern powers decided to fight. A rumour reached the admiral that the defences of the Danes were very strong, and that Copenhagen one of the finest capitals in Europe, was literally bristling with guns. His indecision was overruled by Nelson.

"They will grow stronger every day and ever hour," he cried. "On your decision depends whether our country shall be degraded in the eyes of Europe, or whether she shall rear her head higher than ever."

The die was cast, and the fleet sailed on between the coasts of Denmark and Sweden till the island of Zealand was reached. There were two ways round the island—one by the Sound and Copenhagen, the key to the Baltic, the other by the Belt. Another discussion arose.

"Let it be by the Sound, by the Belt, or any other way," cried Nelson impatiently; "but lose not an hour."

The batteries at Elsinore fired on the ships, but they swept proudly on through the Sound and anchored near Copenhagen. Even Nelson was astonished at the threatening appearance of the enemy's preparations. The Danish ships bristled with cannon, the entrance to the harbour was protected by a chain, and batteries commanded the entrance. It was suggested that the three northern fleets would surely defeat the English at last.

"So much the better," said Nelson excitedly, as he paced the deck of his ship; "I wish there were twice as many. The greater the number, the more glorious the victory."

It was April 1, the night before the battle. Nelson, who had been working hard all day, sat down to dinner with a large party of his officers. He was in the highest spirits.

"To-morrow," he had just written home, "will, I hope, be a proud day for England."

He slept little all night, receiving reports of the wind from hour to hour. When morning dawned it was fair. Every plan was made for the attack.

It was just ten o'clock when the
"Sign of battle flew
O'er the lofty British line:

There was silence deep as death;
And the boldest held his breath

For a time."

Slowly towards the Danish ships, drawn up in line of battle outside Copenhagen, came on the English, until the thunder of guns rolled from end to end of the battle-line. It was a narrow channel, and shallow, and the first English ships ran aground, throwing out all Nelson's plans.

For three hours the fighting continued: the admiral watched with anxiety the growing danger of Nelson's position. The Danes, old sea-rovers as they were, fought with a splendid courage, and fearing for his fleet, the admiral ran up a signal to "Cease action!"

Meanwhile Nelson was pacing his quarter-deck in great excitement.

"It is warm work," he said. "This day may be the last to any of us at any moment. But mark you," he added with feeling, "I would not, be elsewhere for thousands."

Then suddenly from the mast-head of the flag-ship flew the admiral's signal. Nelson did not see it. They told him of it.

"Cease action?" he cried, as if he could not understand. "Fly from the enemy? Never! Never!"

Then turning to one of his officers, he said bitterly, "You know I have only one eye. I have a right to be blind sometimes." With these words he put the telescope to his blind eye, exclaiming with some humour, "I really do not see the signal!"

"Keep my signal flying for closer battle. Nail it to the mast!" he said with emphasis. And the battle raged on fiercely. By two o'clock the Danish fire grew less, and as the smoke cleared away the Danish flagship was seen drifting in flames before the wind, with her miserable crew throwing themselves overboard from every port-hole. The battle was practically over, and again Nelson had won the victory. Under a flag of truce he sent a messenger ashore with terms addressed to "The brothers of Englishmen—the Danes."

"Out spoke the victor then,
As he hail'd them o'er the wave:
'Ye are brothers! we are men!
And we conquer but to save;—
So peace instead of death let us bring:
But yield, proud foe, thy fleet,
With the crews, at England's feet,
And make submission meet
To our king."

"I have been in one hundred and five engagements," said Nelson; "but this is the most terrible of all."

So the Danish fleet was destroyed, and Nelson returned to England the victor of Copenhagen.

24

Napoleon, Emperor of the French

"Who, born no king, made millions draw his car;
Whose game was empires and whose stakes were thrones;
Whose table, earth; whose dice were human bones."
—BYRON.

The dreams of Napoleon, with regard to India, vanished in the thunder and smoke of the battle of the Nile.

"If it had not been for you English," he said, "I should have been Emperor of the East."

A year later, after varied success in Egypt and Syria, he made up his mind to return to France, though the great army must be left behind for the present. One dark night, he embarked in a small ship that had been secretly built, and sailed away along the coast of Africa to Tunis. His voyage was one of great peril, for English ships were patrolling up and down the Mediterranean, and would gladly have fallen in with Napoleon. With all lights out and under cover of the night, the little ship safely accomplished the narrow channel between Sicily and the African coast, and Napoleon reached his old home in Corsica safely.

On October 16, 1799, the citizens of Paris were astounded by the news, that Napoleon was actually among them again. What if he had left them but a year ago, with a magnificent fleet and an army of picked soldiers? He returned alone, but at a time when France stood in need of a strong man.

His arrival inspired all with joy. Men had grown dissatisfied with their Directory. They were ready for a change. Napoleon was at once given command of all the troops in Paris; and, with his military force to support him, he dissolved the Directory and formed a new Government, in which he himself took the highest place. In imitation of the Romans of old, he took the title of Consul. He at once went to live at the palace of the Tuileries. Not a single member of the royal family was left in France, for the little dauphin had died five years before of ill-treatment, and his sister was in exile.

It is curious to remember, that one of Napoleon's first orders as Consul, was to command the French soldiers to wrap their banners in crape, for the death of George Washington in America, for "he was a great man," he said, "who fought against tyranny."

The next object of the Consul, was to reconquer Italy, which had been won back by Austria, during his absence in Egypt. He collected a large force, and, taking command himself, set out as secretly as possible. He knew the Austrians to be encamped in a valley at the foot of Mount St Bernard, a part of the Alps supposed to be impassable.

This famous expedition across the Alps, was one of Napoleon's greatest exploits, and for danger and daring exceeded anything, that had been attempted since the days of Hannibal. With astonishing courage, the French soldiers struggled up the steep and slippery mountain, covered with eternal frost and snow. There was no path. Gallantly they dragged up the cannon, baggage, knapsacks, guns, leading their horses and mules. Amid precipices and glaciers they made their way, across chasm and along airy ridges of rock. And Napoleon himself, dressed in the grey overcoat which had become already famous, cheered on his men, inspiring them with that confidence which had won him so many victories. After seven days' incessant toil they arrived at the end of their goal, and the victory of Marengo repaid them for their tremendous march.

Two months later Napoleon was back in Paris.

"We have done with the romance of the Revolution: we must now begin its history," he said on his return to France.

He was indeed to open that history with an event that affected the whole world, when, in 1804, he was crowned Emperor of France.

Nothing could exceed the magnificence of the ceremony. Napoleon himself was dressed in a French coat of red velvet, embroidered in gold, his collar gleaming with diamonds, over which he wore the long purple robe of velvet and ermine, with a wreath of laurel on his head. His wife, now the Empress Josephine, in white satin glittering with diamonds, was beside him. The Pope had been fetched from Rome to perform the service; but as he was about to crown the Emperor, he was gently waved aside, and Napoleon, with his own hands, crowned himself.

He was more than ever bent now on the conquest of England, and all the forces of his vast empire were brought against her. Great Britain was the one "barrier in the path of his ambition." His plan of invasion was very formidable. He constructed a huge camp at Boulogne. In the port he had 1000 ships built, each to carry 100 soldiers and some guns across the Channel to the coast of Kent.

"Let us be masters of the Straits for six hours," said Napoleon, "and we shall be masters of the world."

So sure was he of success, that he actually had a medal struck of Hercules crushing the sea-monster to commemorate the victory that was never won. There were French fleets in the harbours of Toulon and Brest waiting to help, as well as Spanish ships in the harbour of Cadiz. But for the present these were all closely blockaded by English admirals. There is nothing finer in the naval history of England, than the dogged perseverance with which these dauntless men kept watch. For two years Nelson guarded Toulon, for three years Cornwallis watched the French ships in the harbour of Brest, while Collingwood blockaded a port in the north of Spain. It was these "iron blockades" that thwarted the plans of Napoleon, and saved for England "the realm of the circling sea."

It was not till June 1805, that a general move took place. The French fleet escaped from Toulon, joined the Spaniards at Cadiz, and sailed for the West Indies. Nelson, with ten ships, went off in full pursuit, only to learn on arrival that the French admiral Villeneuve had doubled back towards England. There was no time to lose.

"The fleets of England are equal to meet the world in arms," Nelson said confidently. His words were to prove true when, in October, the fleets met in the last great sea-fight off Trafalgar, which was to decide England's supremacy at sea.

25

The Battle of Trafalgar

"England expects every man to do his duty."
—NELSON'S signal.

The morning of October 21 dawned. It was one of the most important days in the history of the world, for on it, England won her greatest naval victory, and lost her greatest sailor, Lord Nelson.

The sun never rose on a grander scene. Thirty-three French and Spanish ships stretched in a long line covering five miles of sea, off the coast of Spain between Cadiz and Gibraltar. In the distance behind them, Cape Trafalgar was dimly visible in the brightening light against the eastern sky. Towering among the Spanish ships, was the Santissima Trinidad, with her 130 guns, the largest warship afloat, a gleaming mass of red and white. She had escaped the British at Cape St Vincent; she was not going to escape them again. The French and Spanish flagships were there in the midst, Villeneuve being in command of the whole.

The sea was very calm, the lightest of breezes ruffled its surface from time to time, while a long Atlantic swell rolled at intervals towards the straits.

Some ten miles away was the British fleet, numbering twenty-seven ships. It lay in two long columns. At the head of one was Admiral Collingwood on board the Royal Sovereign; at the head of the other was Lord Nelson, the hero of the Nile and Copenhagen, on board the Victory. He had come on deck soon after daybreak,—a "homely figure, slender, stooping, boyish—boyish still in spite of so many battle scars, with the careless hair lying low on his forehead." The empty sleeve of his right arm, his sightless eye, the weather-stained uniform, the orders shining on his breast—all spoke of faithful service to his country. To-day he was to complete that faithful service, by the surrender of his life.

Afraid lest the glitter of his medals should make him too great a mark for his foes, it was suggested to him to remove them.

"In honour I gained them," was the proud answer; "in honour I will die with them."

His plans for the battle had been made long ago. All through the moonless night, his signals had been flashing across the dark waters. He knew the position of the enemy's fleet. The order for sailing had been given, and the decks were being cleared for action, when Nelson withdrew to his cabin. There he was found a little later on his knees, writing, and this is what he wrote: "May the great God whom I worship, grant to my country, and for the benefit of Europe in general, a great and glorious victory; and may no misconduct in any one tarnish it; and may humanity after victory be the predominant feature in the British fleet. For myself, I commit my life to Him who made me, and may His blessing light upon my endeavours for serving my country faithfully. To Him I resign myself and the just cause which is intrusted to me to defend. Amen. Amen. Amen."

The British fleet was heading direct for the foe when Nelson next came on deck. It was about half-past eleven, when flags from the mast-head of the Victory, spelt out to the slowly moving ships Nelson's famous signal—"England expects every man to do his duty." It is said that a shout of approval greeted the admiral's message.

"I can do no more," said Nelson. "I thank God for this great opportunity of doing my duty."

On sailed the British ships in two lines, a mile apart, led by Nelson and Collingwood. They were sailing at right angles to the enemy's line, intending to cut it in two at two points. Nelson's old plan, of arranging for two English ships to attack one French, was at work. The French and Spanish flagships were in the middle of the line, and against them Nelson and Collingwood directed their course.

It was just after noon when a very tempest of shot was poured on to the Victory from eight great battleships around her. Nelson was pacing the deck, with his old friend and comrade Captain Hardy. Suddenly a shot passed between them. Both men started and looked at one another.

"This is too warm work to last long, Hardy," he said, smiling.

The Victory moved on amid tremendous fire. Her sails were riddled with shot, her topmast was falling; but still her guns were silent till, suddenly, she discharged at the French flagship a deafening crash of cannon-balls, which struck down 400 of her men and put twenty guns out of action at once. Moving on her way with dignity, she next attacked a French ship, the Redoubtable. Fiercely raged the battle now along the line. Fiercely fought French and Spanish, none more bravely than the Redoubtable herself. Nothing could exceed the valour of the French on board the little ship, now fighting for her life between the Victory and the Temeraire. With half her masts gone, her hull shot through and through, twenty of her guns out of action and more than half her crew dead or dying, she fought on, with a heroism worthy of victory. It was a shot from her, that killed England's greatest admiral.

He was pacing the deck with Hardy, when quite suddenly he fell, mortally wounded, with his face to the deck.

"They have done for me at last, Hardy," he exclaimed, as the captain picked him up. "My backbone is shot through."

It was true. The shadow of death had been over him all day.

"God bless you, Blackwood," he had said to one of his officers, before the action began; "I shall never speak to you again."

They carried the wounded man below. Bravely he covered his face and medals with a handkerchief that his sailors might not recognise him.

Few stories in history are more pathetic, than this one of the death of Nelson, in the hour of victory. Faithfully every word that fell from the lips of the dying man, has been recorded, until every child now knows the details of those last sad moments.

The Death of Nelson

"Heard ye the thunder of battle
Low in the South and afar?
Saw ye the flash of the death-cloud
Crimson on Trafalgar?
Such another day, never
England will look on again,
Where the battle fought was the hottest
And the hero of heroes was slain."
—PALGRAVE (Trafalgar).

While the thunder of battle roared above, they laid Nelson tenderly on a bed, in the dimly lit cabin below; men lay around, dead and dying.

"You can do nothing for me," he said to the surgeon who bent anxiously over him; "I have but a short time to live."

He was right: the wound was mortal. Nothing could save the precious life, now ebbing away only too fast.

"Pray for me, doctor," whispered Nelson, as the agony of pain threatened to unman him.

Still the battle raged on above. At every cheer that told of victory, a smile passed over the face of the dying man. At last the news came down, that the enemy was all but defeated, and hope was expressed that Nelson would yet live, to bear the grand tidings home to England.

"It is all over: it is all over," was his sorrowful reply.

He longed to see Captain Hardy, who was busy on deck.

"Will no one bring Hardy to me?" he repeated. "He must be killed."

"Oh Victory, Victory," he murmured once as the ship shook to the roar of her guns, "how you distract my poor brain."

At last Hardy snatched a few moments to visit his dying friend. Nelson grasped his hand.

"Well, Hardy, how goes the battle? How goes the day with us?" he cried.

"Very well, my lord," was the reply; "we have got twelve or fourteen of the enemy's ships in our possession."

"I am a dead man, Hardy," he said presently. "I am going fast; it will soon be all over with me."

Hardy bent over his dying friend, then grasped him by the hand, and hurried back to his post on the deck with a bursting heart.

"One would like to live a little longer," Nelson said to the doctor when Hardy had gone.

"My lord," was the heart-broken answer, "unhappily for our country, nothing can be done for you." And he turned away to hide his falling tears.

Another agonised hour passed away. It was four o'clock, when Hardy returned again to the cabin, where Nelson still lay. Grasping his hand, he now announced that the victory was almost complete. Some fifteen ships had been taken.

"That is well," said Nelson; "but I had bargained for twenty."

Then as he planned out the end of the battle, arose a picture of a rising gale, and the battered British fleet perhaps drifting ashore with its prizes.

"Anchor, Hardy, anchor," he said eagerly.

"I suppose, my lord, Admiral Collingwood will now take upon himself the direction of affairs," said Hardy.

"Not while I live, Hardy, I hope," cried Nelson, struggling to raise himself in bed. "No; do you anchor, Hardy."

"Shall we make the signal, sir?"

"Yes; for if I live I'll anchor," was the firm reply.

These were his last commands.

"Kiss me, Hardy," he whispered presently.

Reverently the captain knelt and kissed his cheek.

"Now I am satisfied," murmured Nelson. "Thank God, I have done my duty."

Hardy had risen. He now stood looking silently at the dying Admiral. Suddenly he knelt down and kissed him again.

"Who is that?" asked Nelson.

"It is Hardy," answered his friend.

"God bless you, Hardy," murmured the dying man.

And Hardy then left him—for ever.

About half-past four—three hours after his wound—Nelson died. Before sunset all firing had ceased. The battle of Trafalgar was over.

The news of the two events was received in England with mingled joy and sorrow. "God gave us the victory—but Nelson died," said the people.

Nearly a hundred years have passed away since the famous victory of Trafalgar, when Lord Nelson, Admiral of the British Fleet, was killed. But England's fleet is still her all-in-all; her realm is still the realm of the encircling sea; and the famous signal, "England expects every man to do his duty," rings in her ears to-day.

27

A Second Charlemagne

"When Europe crouched to France's yoke,
And Austria bent and Prussia broke."
—SCOTT.

When the news of Trafalgar reached Napoleon, he had already given up the camp at Boulogne. The thousand ships in the harbour lay forgotten, the relics of a dismal failure. When Villeneuve, after giving Nelson a chase to the West Indies, had made for Cadiz instead of the coast of England, Napoleon's anger had burst forth.

"That Villeneuve," he had cried, choking with rage as he strode up and down his room, "is not fit to command a frigate. What a navy! What an admiral!"

His dreams of invading England by means of India, had vanished in the smoke and thunder of Aboukir Bay. His dreams of invading England herself, disappeared in the roar of the guns at Trafalgar.

But already his active brain was working on an alternate scheme, for bringing that proud nation to his feet. He could not conquer England, but he would conquer Europe. If he could not enter London, he would enter Vienna, the capital of Austria; Berlin, the capital of Prussia; Moscow, the capital of Russia,—all of which countries were at this time allied with England against France. He would conquer these, and so ruin England's trade in Europe; close every port against her, and so reduce her to submission. England was the mistress of the seas, but Napoleon would be master of the land.

In September of 1805 he left Paris for Germany. Already thousands of his troops were silently marching along a hundred roads from Boulogne to the Black Forest, to prevent the union of the allies. They were guided by the master-mind of Napoleon, and they marched to certain victory.

Four days before the battle of Trafalgar, a large Austrian army was compelled to surrender to the French at Ulm, on the banks of the Danube. And while Nelson was preparing for battle off Cape Trafalgar, Napoleon was receiving the homage of the vanquished Austrians, and sending off a waggon-load of Austrian trophies to speak of victory to the people at Paris. This cleared the way to Vienna, which Napoleon entered as a conqueror on November 13.

Three weeks later Russians and Austrians fought side by side at Austerlitz, a small town to the north of Vienna.

"English gold has brought these Russians from the ends of the earth," he told his soldiers. "In twenty-four hours that army will be mine."

The sun rose brightly on December 3, the morning of the battle. It shone on the faces of 73,000 Frenchmen, resolved to conquer or to die; it cast its shadows before the grey colours of the Russians and the white coats of the Austrians, as they pressed forward towards the frozen swamps of the little river that flowed by the town. And the "Sun of Austerlitz" passed into a proverb, as a sure omen for victory. It was the anniversary of Napoleon's coronation, too, and his soldiers cried with enthusiasm, that they would celebrate it in a manner worthy of its glory.

The day wore on, and the two Emperors—Alexander of Russia and Francis of Austria—beheld from the heights of Austerlitz, the complete destruction of their armies. 21,000 Russians and 6000 Austrians lay dead or dying on the field, while guns and banners fell into the hands of the victorious French.

Austerlitz completed, what Ulm had begun. The union of Russia and Austria with England against France, was undone. Undone, also, was the English statesman who had planned the union. The news of the defeat of Austerlitz killed William Pitt. The brilliant son of a brilliant father, Pitt had played a large part in his country during the French Revolution and the rise of Napoleon to power.

"It is not a chip of the old block,—it is the old block itself," Burke had cried, when young Pitt had made one of his first speeches in the English House of Commons. He had loved England with all the fierce devotion of his father, the Earl of Chatham. He had refused to bow to the dictates of Napoleon. He had roused England to put forth her full strength to withstand the world-conqueror. He was "the pilot that weathered the storm." His last hopes for England lay in the help of Russia and Austria. Now that help was gone. He was already worn out with work and anxiety; the hollow voice and wasted form had long told his friends that death was not far off. But now the news of Austerlitz killed him. He never recovered from the blow. The terrible "Austerlitz look," as it has been called, never left his face again.

"Roll up that map," he said, his eyes falling on a map of Europe that hung in the house; "it will not be wanted these ten years."

"My country! How I leave my country," he murmured, as he lay dying in the new year of 1806.

"England has saved herself by her exertions, and will, I trust, save Europe by her example."

These famous words he left as a legacy to the country which he had loved long and passionately.

And still the mighty shadow of Napoleon crept on over the map of Europe. England had no Nelson now to conquer on the seas, no Pitt to lift up his voice in her council halls; and the great conqueror carried all before him. He had already made the Emperor of Austria renounce for ever the title of Roman Emperor, which had come down to him through the long ages of the past. It had been bestowed upon Charlemagne by the Pope nearly a thousand years before. It was now cancelled by a second Charlemagne, who ruled over an empire yet greater than the hero of the Middle Ages. The Pope was still sovereign of Rome, but "I am the Emperor!" cried Napoleon. "I do not intend the court of Rome to mix any longer in questions of the world. I am Charlemagne—the Emperor."

On October 14, 1806, the victory of Jena over the Prussians laid North Germany at his feet. As he had entered Vienna a year ago, so now he entered Berlin—a conqueror. Marching on into the heart of Poland, he now defeated the last foe left him in Europe. The summer of 1807 found him dictating peace to Alexander of Russia.

A famous meeting between the two Emperors took place on a raft moored on the river Niemen, at Tilsit.

"I hate the English as much as you do," said Alexander, as he embraced the conqueror Napoleon.

"If that is the case," answered Napoleon, "peace is made."

By this peace of Tilsit, Russia, Austria, and Prussia agreed with France, to close their ports against British trade.

"England," cried Napoleon triumphantly, "sees her merchandise repelled by all Europe, and her ships, loaded with useless wealth, seek in vain a port open to receive them."

Had he succeeded, the history of the world had indeed been changed.

28

The Rise of Wellington

"This is he that far away
Against the myriads of Assaye
Clash'd with his fiery few and won."
—TENNYSON (Wellington).

For the moment it seemed as if the genius of Napoleon would triumph over England herself. But she was now to find herself armed against him by one of her greatest soldiers,—none other than the famous Duke of Wellington,—who should make her almost as strong by land as Nelson had made her at sea. The same year that Napoleon was born in Corsica, a son was born to Wellesley, Earl of Mornington, in Ireland. He was called Arthur. Little enough is known of Arthur Wellesley's childhood.

"I vow to God," his mother exclaimed in the strong language of the day, "I don't know what I shall do with my awkward son Arthur."

At the age of eleven he was sent to school at Eton, in England, where we get a glimpse of his first fight. One of his boy friends was bathing one day in the river Thames, when Arthur Wellesley took up a clod and threw it at him for fun. "If you do that again, I will get out and thrash you," cried the bather angrily. To tease him, the small boy Arthur threw another and yet another. The bather then landed and struck Wellesley. A sharp fight began, in which the smaller boy, Wellesley, easily won.

At the age of twelve, he was taken to Brussels by his mother. Here he learnt music, and little else. He played well on the fiddle, but displayed no other talent. In after years, when he was in India, he used to amuse himself by playing on the fiddle, till suddenly one day it occurred to him, that it was not a very soldier-like calling, and he threw his instrument into the fire.

His mother soon came to the conclusion that her "ugly son Arthur" was "fit food for powder, and nothing more." So he was sent to a military school in France, where he studied at the same time that Napoleon Bonaparte was training for a soldier in the same country. On Christmas Day, 1787, Arthur Wellesley became a lieutenant in an English infantry regiment. He was still a shy, awkward lad, in whom no one saw anything attractive. One night at a large ball, being unable to find a partner to dance with, he sat down near the band to listen to the music. When the party broke up and the other officers went home after a gay and happy evening, young Wellesley was left to travel home with the fiddlers. When in after years he became a great man, his hostess said to him, laughing, "We should not let you go home with the fiddlers now!"

When he was twenty-one, he got a seat in the Irish Parliament, which then sat in Dublin.

"Who is that young man in scarlet uniform with large epaulettes?" asked a visitor to the Irish House of Commons.

"That is Captain Wellesley," was the reply.

"I suppose he never speaks."

"You are wrong," was the answer; "he does speak. And when he does, it is always to the point."

Wellesley began his Indian career in 1797. Matters in the East were once more in a critical condition. Tippoo, Governor of Mysore, son of Britain's old foe Hyder Ali, was in secret correspondence with Napoleon for driving the English out of India.

"I am coming to help you drive the English out of the country," Napoleon had written to Tippoo, as he started for Egypt on his way to India. The battle of Aboukir Bay put an end to that promise; but Tippoo's attitude was very threatening, and against him, young Wellesley was now sent in command of troops. At Seringapatam, the capital of Mysore, Tippoo was defeated and slain. Wellesley was made Commander of the Forces in Mysore, with power over the whole dominion of Mysore, till the little new five-year-old Raja was older. For the next two years he worked hard in Mysore, bringing the country into order, until early in 1803 he was given command of a large number of troops, with orders to march against one of the Rajas who was threatening the English frontiers. The rising was assuming a very alarming size when Wellesley encountered the enemy, strongly posted behind the river Kaitna, near the village of Assaye. His troops were tired with a long march, and the meeting was unexpected. He must either fight at once or retreat. He resolved to fight, though the force against him numbered some 50,000 men and 128 guns, as opposed to his 8000 men and 17 guns. It was a great decision. It was his first great battle. The native guides assured him, that it was impossible to cross the river; the banks were steep and rocky, and there was no ford. But Wellesley made up his mind to take the risk. It was a breathless moment, when the advance-guard reached the river. The Highlanders plunged in, and suspense gave way to triumph, as Wellesley saw them half across with the water only waist high. Shot ploughed the water around, them, but bravely they reached the farther bank, and a sharp conflict ensued. Wellesley himself was in the thick of the action the whole time, giving his orders as coolly as an experienced veteran. His horse was shot under him, but he mounted another and fought on. By evening the enemy was in full retreat. Wellesley was victorious on the field of Assaye. He had crushed the rebellion, and secured to England her dominions.

For this he received the thanks of Parliament and a sword of honour from Calcutta, being also made a knight—a great honour in those days, when there were but twenty-four.

His brother was now Governor-General of India, for which country a new era of prosperity had now begun. In the course of seven years British power was established all over India. But better than this, the brothers Wellesley put an end to the corrupt practices, that had ended the rule of Warren Hastings so miserably. Under them a new rule of honour and justice began for India, which is carried on by England to-day.

Sir Arthur Wellesley now returned to England. He had left home eight years before, a young officer little known, less admired. He returned, having won his spurs and earned for himself fame and honour. He arrived just a month before Nelson started to fight his last great sea-fight at Trafalgar. For a few minutes only, the two men met—young Wellesley on the threshold of a career, which was to end in so much glory, and Lord Nelson, whose famous career was so nearly drawing to its close.

29

At the Cape of Good Hope

"I hear the sound of pioneers,
Of nations yet to be."
—WHITTIER.

The capture of the Cape of Good Hope was an important result of the battles of Camperdown and Trafalgar. The first of these destroyed the sea power of Holland, the second secured it to England.

Slowly but surely the little colony founded by Van Riebeek at the Cape had grown and prospered. Let us take up its story from those early days.

For some time, the colonists had been content to stay under the shadow of Table Mountain, but as the years passed on, the younger colonists became adventurous. Musket in hand, to drive back the native Hottentots of the country, they began to explore inland, until little settlements sprang up in all directions. They were presently joined by some 300 French Huguenots, who had been driven from their country and taken refuge in Holland. At first these people clung to their French language and service of the French church, but soon the Dutch forbade this, and they talked and worshipped with their neighbours. Not long after their arrival, a terrible outbreak of smallpox swept whole tribes of Hottentots away, and the inland country was clear for the European colonists. Farther and farther inland now they spread, over the mountains to the pasture land beyond. The grass was thin, and it was necessary to graze the cattle over wide stretches of ground. Thus they became more and more cut off from the coast and from the far-off homes of their ancestors. With their wives and children they followed the cattle from spot to spot: their children were untaught, their wives forgot the neat and cleanly ways of their Dutch forefathers. At last they reached the Great Fish River and came in contact with the Kaffirs. These were the natives, who occupied the lands from the Zambesi to the Great Fish River. They consisted of a number of tribes, constantly making war on each other, who appear later under various names of Zulus, Swazis, and Basutos.

All the colonists fretted under the misrule of the Dutch East India Company. They were worried with petty laws and obliged to pay heavy taxes; the farmers were told exactly what to grow, and forced to give up much of their produce. The company had broken faith with the natives, and had imported a number of slaves into the colony, which had no need of negro labour. When, therefore, in the year 1795 the news spread, that English troops were in possession of Cape Town, the idea of change was not wholly unwelcome. The English came as friends of the Dutch, in their united struggle against the French. The Prince of Orange was an exile in England, and the English carried a letter from him to the Dutch officials at the Cape.

Conquerors and conquered came of the same stock. Of all the nations in Europe, the people of Holland are closest to those of Great Britain. True, 1400 years of separation had altered the history of each, but many points of resemblance were left. Both were a liberty-loving people, both were Protestant, both had Viking blood in their veins. Moreover, it was as simple for the Dutchman to learn English, as it was for the Englishman to learn Dutch. Here is a quaint picture, of how the colonists from the surrounding districts came into Cape Town, to take the oath of allegiance to George III. of England.

Over the Dutch castle flew the English flag. Within was the English governor. The gates stood open. First came the Dutch officials, all dressed in black, "well-fed, rosy-cheeked men with powdered hair." They walked in pairs with their hats off. They were followed by the Boers or farmers, who had come in from distant parts of the colony. They were splendid men, head and shoulders above their neighbours, and broad in proportion. They were dressed in blue cloth jackets and trousers and tall flat hats. Behind each, crept a black Hottentot servant, carrying his master's umbrella. The Hottentot was small: he wore a sheepskin round his shoulders, and a hat trimmed with ostrich feathers.

For nearly eight years, the English ruled. Then came another peace between France and England after the battle of Copenhagen, by which the Cape was given back to Holland, now subject to France. The old Dutch East India Company had by this time disappeared, for since the battle of Camperdown, Holland had lost command of the sea. For the next three years, the Cape was hers again. Africa is a land of surprises: once more she was to change hands.

The Cape had been "swept into the whirlpool" of the European conflict raging with Napoleon. More than ever now, England felt the importance of possessing the Cape as a naval stronghold, as a half-way house to her ever-increasing dominions in India. The power of the sea was now hers beyond dispute. The victory of Trafalgar made all things possible. So she sent an expedition to South Africa. Early in the new year of 1806, sixty-three English ships came sweeping into Table Bay. But a gale was blowing, and the heavy surf rolling in to the shore, made landing impossible for a time. The Dutch prepared to defend Cape Town, but they had not the means or the men. It was the height of summer, and the Boers of the country could not leave their farms.

So the English took the Cape, and once again the British flag flew from the top of the castle ramparts.

A few years later the English occupation was acknowledged, and Holland sold her rights for the sum of £6,000,000.

The English governors were men of high character, and anxious for the welfare of the new colony. Reforms were introduced, schools were built, the slave-trade was forbidden, justice administered. The Dutch law was allowed to remain as it was, and it is to-day the common law of all the British colonies in South Africa.

It seemed as if an era of peace and prosperity were about to begin, and there seemed no reason why the history of the happy union of English and Dutch at New York, in America, should not repeat itself.

30

The First Australian Colony

"Look, I have made ye a place and opened wide the doors."
—KIPLING.

Beyond the Cape of Good Hope and across the wide Pacific lay Australia, the Great South Land, still occupied only by wandering native tribes. But now, as men pored over the thrilling journals of Captain Cook, they felt that "a new earth was open in the Pacific for the expansion of the English race."

The independence of America, had made the plantations no longer possible for English convict settlements, so it was decided to use the new empty continent-island, in the distant Pacific, for this purpose. In the year 1788, the first fleet of eleven ships anchored off Botany Bay, on the eastern coast of Australia, after eight months at sea. Some 800 convicts were on board under Governor Phillips.

The landing-place proved disappointing, and in an open rowing-boat Phillips explored northwards. Port Jackson fulfilled all requirements.

"Here," wrote the governor triumphantly home—"Here we have the satisfaction of finding the finest harbour in the world, in which a thousand sail of the line may ride in perfect safety."

In honour of Lord Sydney, Secretary of State in England, he named the chosen spot Sydney, and here to-day stands one of the most important towns in Australia. Soon the British flag was waving over the tents and huts of the settlers, and New South Wales was declared British territory, from Cape Howe, in the south, to Cape York, its most northern extremity.

"What Frobisher and Raleigh did for America, we are to-day doing for Australia," cried the governor with enthusiasm, to his little band of pioneers.

But, like other early settlements, this one was doomed to suffer. Misfortunes fell thick on the little colony. A drought set in: the seeds did not sprout. The cattle disappeared, the sheep died. Store-ships from England were wrecked. And still more and more convicts were sent out.

"We have not a shoe to our feet nor a shirt to our backs," wrote the wretched colonists. Famine stared them in the face.

Yet in the colony's darkest hour the governor never swerved from his opinion. "This country," he repeats, "will prove the most valuable acquisition Great Britain ever made."

Cheerfully he shared the slender daily rations with the convicts. But the time came, when even they were nearly finished. Phillips watched in vain for a friendly sail on the horizon. "At times," he says pathetically, "when the day was fast setting and the shadows of the evening stretched out, I have been deceived by some fantastic little cloud resembling the sails of a ship."

At last it came. Men wrung each other's hands with overflowing hearts, women kissed their children with passionate tears of relief. The colony was saved. But the governor was broken down with long anxiety, and had to return to England.

On board the new vessel bringing the new governor, were two young men, thirsting for adventure. Their names—Bass and Flinders—are now famous in the annals of Australian discovery. No sooner had they arrived, than they set forth in a little boat only eight feet long, suitably called the Tom Thumb. They followed the coast of New South Wales for a considerable distance, making clear much that was obscure. Then Bass got a whale-boat and crew of six men, to proceed on a more important voyage of discovery to the south. It was successful beyond all expectation. He discovered that Tasmania was an island, and the channel that separates it from the mainland has since borne the name of Bass's Straits. He had sailed 600 miles in his whale-boat through boisterous storms, and he returned to Sydney to find himself a hero. His achievement ranked as one of the boldest in the annals of navigation.

Soon after this, Flinders, in command of the Investigator, sailed completely round the coast of Australia. Starting from King George's Sound, in the extreme south-west, he passed by the bleak rocky heights of the Great Australian Bight, naming bays and islands as he sailed. On the map to-day we find "Investigator Islands" and "Investigator Straits." There, too, is Cape Catastrophe, where the ship's master was drowned, owing to the capsizing of the boat in which he was landing. Kangaroo Island was discovered by him, and so called because it was a very "kangaroo paradise." These quiet brown animals were so tame, that it was easy enough to kill them, and the ship's crew had a splendid feast after long privations on board. Encounter Bay speaks of his meeting with French ships, also exploring the coast of Australia; and Port Phillip, named after the first Australian governor, was soon to become famous for the city of Melbourne, which stands there to-day.

After a rest at Sydney the energetic Flinders set forth again. He sailed round the northern territory, which in 1863 was added to the province of South Australia, and returned to Sydney after another year's absence.

It would take too long to tell the adventures that befell Flinders, on his way back to England; how he set sail and was wrecked on the great coral reef, which bars the north-east coast of New South Wales; how he found a small boat of twenty-nine tons, in which he sailed safely across the ocean to Mauritius, where he was taken prisoner by the French, then in possession. For six years he lay in captivity, till Trafalgar had been fought and won, and Mauritius fell into English hands. Two more tragedies ended his life. The French had already published an account of Australian explorations and his own account was published the very day he died.

So far most of the exploration of the great south continent had been by sea. No white man had ventured far inland. For some sixty miles inland, running parallel to the east coast, rose the chain of the Blue Mountains. With their jagged peaks and bottomless chasms, they had so far proved an impassable barrier to the interior. Even the daring Bass had tried and failed. He had climbed precipices with iron hooks fastened to his arms, and descended into terrific caverns by means of ropes, but he had not been able to accomplish the feat of gaining the other side.

It now became a matter of extreme importance to extend the boundaries of New South Wales inland. Shipload after shipload of colonists had sailed from the mother country, till more pasturage was required for the ever increasing flocks and herds. At last three colonists started off, determined to force a way through the Blue Mountains. Bound together by ropes and armed with axes, they cut their way bravely through the virgin forests, climbing as they went. Forward and upward they fought their way, where no white man had penetrated before, past the spot, where Bass had failed, till they discovered a range, along the ridge of which they made their way. Arrived at the last summit, they were rewarded by the magnificent prospect, that now opened before them. They had seen their promised land, and the three ragged hungry pioneers made their way back to Sydney with their joyful news. The discovery meant new life to the colony, and two years later, just before the battle of Waterloo, a road was triumphantly opened across the Blue Mountains, to the famous plains of Bathurst.

It was no wonder that Kendall, the poet of New South Wales, broke into song over this famous exploit.

"The dauntless three. For twenty days and nights
These heroes battled with the haughty heights;
For twenty spaces of the star and sun
These Romans kept their harness buckled on;
By gaping gorges, and by cliffs austere,
These fathers struggled in the great old year;

Their feet they set on strange hills scarred by fire,
Their strong arms forced a path through brake and briar;
They fought with Nature till they reached the throne
Where morning glittered on the Great Unknown."

31

Story of the Slave-trade

"When a deed is done for freedom,
through the broad earth's aching breast
Runs a thrill of joy prophetic,
trembling on from east to west,
And the slave, where'er he cowers,
feels the soul within him climb
To the awful verge of manhood,
as the energy sublime
Of a century bursts full-blossomed
on the thorny stem of time."
—LOWELL.

When the English took over the Cape of Good Hope from the Dutch, there were a larger number of negro slaves there, than white men.

Let us take up the story of the slave-trade, and see how Great Britain took the lead in stopping this deplorable labour market, which she had been among the first to start.

From the earliest times, there had been slaves. Abraham had his slaves, the Greeks had slaves, and the Romans had slaves. They were prisoners of war, kept as bondsmen by their conquerors, and thus deprived of freedom. Thus, when the Romans conquered Britain, we get the well-known story of the little British slaves, in the market-place at Rome.

One day the Bishop of Rome noted the fair faces, white bodies, and golden hair of the small boys who stood bound in the slave market, waiting to be sold.

"From what country do these come?" he asked the slave-dealers.

"They are English—Angles," they told him.

"Not Angles, but Angels," commented the bishop, "with faces so angel-like."

"What is the name of their king?" he asked.

"Ælla," was the answer.

"Alleluia shall be sung in Ælla's land," he cried.

As Christianity spread, the condition of the slaves grew better, and gradually this sort of slavery vanished.

But in the fifteenth century, slavery again grew and flourished.

When the Portuguese, under Prince Henry the Navigator, were exploring the coast of West Africa, they one day brought back some black men, to show their royal master. The first idea in those days was to make these black men Christian, and to use them in the royal household. They were very useful, and more and more ships went off to the west coast, to bring back to Spain and Portugal these negroes. When Columbus discovered the West Indies, these black men were shipped over from Africa in quantities, to take the place of the native Indians in the sugar plantations. Presently the supply of negroes from the coast was exhausted, and men had to go inland and hunt them down to the coast. The first Englishman to engage in this cruel traffic was Captain John Hawkins, of Elizabethan fame. In the year 1562, he sailed to Sierra Leone, where he captured 300 negroes, which he sold for high prices to the Spaniards in the West Indies.

These were days of adventure and daring, in which human suffering played a large, silent part. Hawkins thought nothing of setting fire to native villages in Africa, and capturing the negroes as they attempted to escape. They were then chained together, as though they had been cattle, and driven to the coast to wait for ships bound for America. In the small sailing ships of the day, they were crammed below close to one another, as herrings in a barrel. In this state, they had to toss on the high seas for weeks together. Hundreds of them died from cold, exposure, want of proper food, and disease, before ever they reached the new homes of their bondage. They were gratefully bought by the colonists in America, for labourers were scarce, and there was much to be done in the new country.

Dutch and French joined in the trade. Each nation had its own slave centre in West Africa, and each shipped negro slaves to its own colony, on the distant shores of the Atlantic Ocean. As the demand increased, so the supply increased, till the slave-trade became the very life of the new colonies, the "strength and sinews" of the Western world.

Soon more than half the trade was in British hands. From Liverpool and Bristol, nearly 200 ships sailed in the course of one year, to pick up slaves in Africa to sell in America.

It was not till the eighteenth century, that the nature of the slave-trade came to be understood, when stories of cruelty and misery endured by the slaves, reached Europe, and all that was best in England rose up against it. Men began to inquire more into the condition of the slave. They learnt that he was treated as an animal, rather than a human being.

"A slave"—ran the slave-dealer's contract—"a slave is in the power of the master to whom he belongs. The master may sell him, dispose of his person, his industry, his labour. He can do nothing, possess nothing, nor acquire anything, but what must belong to his master."

This was slavery indeed. Further, his children might be torn from him and sold to other masters, and he reaped no reward from the long and weary days of work often forced from him by means of a whip. Of course there were exceptions. There were slaves devoted to their masters, slaves who would die for them. But, as a rule, they were just so many cattle, and treated as such.

The same year that America made her great Declaration of Independence, England declared that the "slave-trade was contrary to the laws of God and the rights of men," and it was decided, that as soon as a slave set his foot on the soil of the British Islands, he was a free man. But it was more than thirty years, before British merchants could be brought to agree to give up this large source of profit. It was not till the year 1807, that the trade was finally forbidden. Meanwhile Denmark had already abolished the slave-trade in her colonies. Gradually the other nations of Europe followed the lead. And so the slave-trade became illegal under the flags of the Western nations. The greatest slave-dealing nation—even freedom-loving England—had lifted up her voice against oppression and cruelty, had carried her point against tremendous opposition.

"O thou great Wrong, that through the slow-paced years
Didst hold thy millions fettered, and didst wield
The scourge that drove the labourer to the field
And turned a stony gaze on human tears,
Thy cruel reign is o'er."

32

The Defence of Saragoza

"Her lover sinks—she sheds no ill-timed tear;
Her chief is slain—she fills his fatal post;
Her fellows flee—she checks their base career;
The foe retires—she heads the sallying host."
—BYRON.

While the world, growing more human, was raising its voice against slavery abroad, Napoleon was turning his attention to Portugal, the traditional friend of Great Britain. He sent a force to invade Portugal, and her capital Lisbon was soon occupied by the French. Now Spain must be conquered too; Spain, with her many valuable possessions in South America, must be added to the growing empire of Napoleon.

On the throne of Spain, was an old and now almost imbecile king, Charles IV., a descendant of Louis XIV. of France. His son, Ferdinand, was little better than himself, and the court of Madrid was a mass of intrigue and scandal.

Napoleon himself travelled to Bayonne, a town on the borders of France and Spain. Here he stopped, and sent for the royal family of Spain. Charles and his queen arrived with the rebellious Ferdinand. Angry scenes took place. The old king brandished his stick over the head of Ferdinand. At last he was persuaded to abdicate his tottering throne in favour of Napoleon, and retire on a pension to France. There was still Ferdinand to be settled.

"Unless between this and midnight you too abdicate," roared Napoleon to the young man, "you shall be treated as a rebel."

Ferdinand was terrified into yielding. Napoleon was triumphant. He had bought the crown of Spain and all her possessions. It was a masterpiece of skill. It was also a tremendous blunder: he did not know the Spanish people. Such high-handed conduct goaded them to madness.

When the news became known, that Joseph Bonaparte had been made King of Spain, one general heart-broken cry rang from end to end of the Peninsula. Then, like a volcano, all Spain burst forth in an explosion of fury and indignation. In one day, in one hour, without signal, without watchword, the whole nation rose, as one man, to withstand the power of Napoleon. From the mountaineers of Asturias in the north, to the sailors of Carthagena in the south, from the Pyrenees to the sea-coast of Portugal, the battle-cry rang out, as, with the pride of ancient Rome, the Spaniards prepared fiercely to defend their country. The story of how they defended Saragoza, is one of the most famous in the history of the world.

Saragoza, the capital of Aragon, was one of the oldest cities of Spain. The very name—Cæsar Augustus—speaks of Roman times. The town stood in an open plain, covered with olive grounds and closed in by high mountains. Standing on the river Ebro, it was entered by twelve gates. It was built wholly of brick: the streets were narrow and crooked. When the French soldiers began to besiege the town in the end of June 1808, there were but a few hundred Spanish soldiers there, sixteen cannon, and a few muskets. But the citizens themselves, under their leader Palafox, set to work to defend their town. They placed beams of timber together, endways, against the houses, in a sloping direction, behind which the people might shelter themselves, when the shot fell. To strengthen their defences, they tore down the awnings of their windows and formed them into sacks, which they filled with sand and piled up before the gates to serve as a battery. All the women helped. They formed themselves into companies—some to nurse the wounded, some to carry food and water to the brave defenders. Monks bore arms, and nuns made cartridges for children to distribute.

Among the heroic defenders was Augustina Saragoza, a young woman of twenty-two. She arrived one day to bring food to the defenders at one of the gates, to find every man had been shot dead, so terrific was the fire from the French guns. Among the dead artillerymen was her lover, so says the story. So desperate was the scene, that for a moment even the Spaniards seemed to waver before they remanned the guns. Augustina sprang forward over the dead and dying, snatched a match from the hands of her dead lover, and fired off a 26-pounder. Then, jumping upon the gun, she swore she would never quit it alive, while the siege lasted. Such heroism put fresh courage into all hearts. The Spaniards rushed into the battery, renewed their fire, and repulsed the French. Augustina kept her word. She was the heroine of a fight, where all were heroines, and she is known to history as the Maid of Saragoza. At the end of forty-six days, the city was completely surrounded, food was failing, and no place was safe from the enemy's fire. On August 2 the hospital took fire, and again the courage of the women was shown, as they carried the sick and wounded men from the beds and fought their way through the burning flames. Two days later the French forced their way into the town and occupied a large convent called St Engracia. The French general then summoned Palafox to surrender.

"Headquarters, St Engracia. Capitulation," was the brief message.

"Headquarters, Saragoza. War to the knife," was the heroic reply.

Terrible was the conflict now the French were in the town. The war raged not only from street to street, but from house to house, from room to room, for eleven days and nights. Stories of heroism are too numerous to tell. A Spaniard managed with difficulty to fasten a rope round one of the French cannon, but in the struggle that ensued, the rope broke, and the prize was lost at the moment of victory. By August 13, little of their city was left to the Spaniards, and things seemed at their worst when, early one morning, the French were seen in full retreat. The men and women of Saragoza had saved their town. True, it was taken by the French after another terrible siege, but the famous courage of the Spaniards was spoken of throughout Europe, and their spirit of patriotism helped to bring them that help from England, which, after years of fighting, freed their country from Napoleon.

33

Sir John Moore at Coruna

"Slowly and sadly we laid him down,
From the field of his fame fresh and gory;
We carved not a line, and we raised not a stone,
But we left him alone with his glory."
—CHARLES WOLFE.

Meanwhile Napoleon was rejoicing in this new addition to his great empire. With the gold of Mexico, he would build a new fleet to rival England on the seas.

"England is mine," he had told himself already, "there is nothing to fear."

But in reality there was much to fear. England had taken up the cause of the Peninsula against him, and Sir Arthur Wellesley was already landing on the coast of Portugal with British troops. With these, he drove the French out of Portugal, and leaving Sir John Moore in his place, he returned to England.

Napoleon now saw that he would have to conquer Spain for himself, and accordingly he left Paris at the head of a large army in the autumn of 1808. In a week he had reached Bayonne, and soon the many passes of the Pyrenees were filled with the ceaseless flow of armed men marching under the banner of the Imperial French eagle.

"When I shall show myself beyond the Pyrenees, the English, in terror, will plunge into the ocean to avoid shame, defeat, and death," said the great warrior, with confidence.

In four divisions, the great French army burst into Spain, carrying all before them, and on December 4th Napoleon entered Madrid in triumph.

"I will drive the English from the Peninsula," he said grandly, as he made his plans for marching on Lisbon and the south of Spain with a tried army of 300,000 men.

"If Spain is not submissive, I shall give my brother another throne and put the crown of Spain on my own head," he announced at Madrid.

But the daring resolve of a British soldier, was now to save Spain from the ever-tightening grip of Napoleon.

Sir John Moore was already marching from Lisbon towards Madrid, when he heard of Napoleon's advance in person. To go on now seemed madness; to retreat without striking a blow, was to betray Spain and dishonour England. Calmly he decided to try and cut off Napoleon's communications, keeping a road for his own retreat to Coruna always open, whence he could embark for England.

This changed the plans of Napoleon. He set out in all haste to meet the English. It was three days before Christmas, when Napoleon and his French troops found themselves at the foot of the Guadamar hills, which lay to the north of Madrid, between him and the English army. Deep snow choked the passes, a storm of wild sleet and snow was raging over the mountains. The night was very dark. The advance-guard pronounced the way to be impossible. "But neither the deep snow nor the wild hills, nor the yet wilder tempest, could stay Napoleon's vehement purpose." Placing himself at the head of the army, he advanced on foot, leading the soldiers through the darkness, amid storms of blinding hail and drifting snow.

The army emerged, after two days' struggle, to find themselves just twelve hours too late to meet Moore and his army. He was already on the way to Coruna. Marshal Soult, one of Napoleon's most famous generals, was in hot pursuit. At the same time Moore was yet some 200 miles from the coast. Soult was pressing him hard: Napoleon was coming up like a tempest behind him.

Christmas passed. The new year of 1809 broke to find Moore and the English still retreating, but Napoleon had given up the pursuit to Soult.

"The English are running away as fast as they can: they fly in terror," he wrote from the town of Astorga, feeling Spain was already his.

Meanwhile Moore was hurrying on. The road lay through wild ranges of hills, for the most part covered with snow. Storms raged around them, the rivers and little streams were swollen, there was no shelter from the deadly blasts of winter. Now and then they turned at bay, hoping that the French, who were on their very heels, would attack. Often through the long dark nights they struggled on, their feet bleeding, their clothes torn,—hungry, thirsty, out of spirits.

At last they straggled into Coruna. They had lost 4000 men from cold and sickness, but not a flag or a gun. Three days' wait and the ships were ready to take them home. Orders for embarking had been given, when the French army, under Soult, was seen moving on the hills, above the town. As Sir John Moore saw what it meant, his face lit up. He might yet retrieve the tragedy of his enforced retreat, yet bring glory to the English arms.

Soon the battle began, and was raging furiously, when Moore was struck by a cannon ball, which threw him from his horse and shattered his shoulder to pieces. Raising himself from the ground on his right elbow, not a moan escaped him, as he eagerly watched the struggle. It was not until he saw that the English were gaining ground, that he suffered himself to be borne away. One of his officers, Hardinge, began to unbuckle his sword, but Moore stopped him.

"It is well as it is," he murmured. "I had rather it should go out of the field with me."

Every now and then he made the soldiers stop, halt, and turn round, so that he might see for himself how the fight was going. Those around him expressed the hope, that he might yet recover.

"No, Hardinge," he said, looking at his terrible wounds; "I feel that to be impossible."

One among the little group burst into tears.

"My friend," said Moore, turning to him with a smile, "this is nothing."

The surgeons who examined him at once saw there was no hope.

"You know I have always wished to die this way," whispered the dying man. "I hope the people of England will be satisfied. I hope my country will do me justice," he added.

And as night fell and the thunder of battle grew fainter and more faint, the hero of Coruna passed away at the hour of victory. Let the well-known lines by Wolfe finish the story.

"Not a drum was heard, not a funeral note,
As his corpse to the ramparts we hurried;
Not a soldier discharged his farewell shot
O'er the grave where our hero we buried.
We buried him darkly at dead of night,
The sods with our bayonets turning,
By the struggling moonbeam's misty light,
And the lanthorn dimly burning.
Few and short were the prayers we said,
And we spoke not a word of sorrow;
But we steadfastly gazed on the face that was dead.
And we bitterly thought of the morrow.
We thought, as we hollow'd his narrow bed
And smooth'd down his lonely pillow,
That the foe and the stranger would tread o'er his head,
And we far away on the billow!
Lightly they'll talk of the spirit that's gone,
And o'er his cold ashes upbraid him;
But little he'll reck, if they let him sleep on
In the grave where a Briton has laid him."

34

The Victory of Talavera

"Greatest, yet with least pretence,
Great in council and great in war,
Foremost captain of his time,
Rich in saving common-sense,
And, as the greatest only are,
In his simplicity sublime."
—TENNYSON (Wellington);

While Sir John Moore lay dying on the field of Coruna, Napoleon was galloping off with all speed to Austria. But he left orders with his generals, that they were to finish driving the English from the Peninsula and subdue the country. He made not the slightest doubt, that all would soon be accomplished, and that his brother Joseph would rule undisturbed over his new Spanish kingdom. But as Sir Arthur Wellesley once more stepped upon the scene, the eyes of Europe became riveted upon the conflict, that now threatened to overthrow that power.

It was but three months after Coruna, that the greatest soldier England could now produce landed at Lisbon. Three French armies, under tried generals, confronted him in Portugal and Spain. It was against Soult at Oporto, that Wellesley determined to strike his first blow. So he marched northwards till he came to the river Douro, which rolled rapidly between him and the enemy at Oporto. The march had been quick, and Soult was strangely unprepared for what now happened. Mounting a hill opposite the town, Wellesley hastily surveyed the situation. There was no bridge over the Douro, no boats visible on the banks. But the river must be crossed. Presently it was discovered, that a barber from Oporto was crossing over in a tiny boat. This was instantly seized, and, springing in, an English officer rowed back across the stream to the farther bank, where he found four old barges stranded in the mud, which he towed across.

"Let the men embark," said Wellesley hastily.

As the English dragged their guns up the hill on the opposite side, Soult discovered what had happened. He had been completely surprised, and nothing was left him, but to retreat with all the speed possible. At four o'clock in the afternoon, it is said that Wellesley ate the dinner prepared for Marshal Soult in Oporto.

With Soult in full flight, and Oporto, the second town in Portugal, in English hands, Wellesley determined to push on towards Madrid. The Spanish army under old Cuesta now joined him; but Cuesta proved a sore trial to the English commander. On June 27 the English and Spanish armies entered Spain, and Wellesley's troubles began. He had crossed the boundary with the full assurance that food should be found for his troops. But Spanish promises proved to be worthless, and the English were nearly starved. Horses died by hundreds, and the British soldiers were led on, complaining bitterly of their treatment. At last they reached Talavera, a picturesque old town on the Tagus, some seventy-five miles to the south of Madrid. Cuesta now proved hopeless. While Wellesley was discussing matters of the highest importance with him, the old man would fall asleep. On July 22, Wellesley found that a single French army was within striking distance, and Cuesta at last agreed to attack him next day, before other French troops joined him. Wellesley was arranging the plan of battle for the morrow, when the old Spanish general rose and went off to bed. The British were under arms at three next morning, but Cuesta did not get up till seven. Then he arrived at the British camp in a coach with six horses, to say that, as it was Sunday, he must decline to fight. Later in the day, he was induced to examine the ground for the coming battle; but he soon alighted from his coach-and-six, sat down under the shade of a neighbouring tree, and went off to sleep.

"If Cuesta had fought, when I wanted him, it would have been as great a battle as Waterloo, and would have cleared the French out of Spain," said Sir Arthur Wellesley pitifully, when speaking of Talavera.

Cuesta's obstinacy cost him dear. Three French armies now joined forces—making some 50,000 in all—and held the road to Madrid. Among the French leaders was Joseph Bonaparte, fighting for his kingdom.

At two o'clock on the afternoon of July 27 the battle of Talavera began. Perhaps the chief feature in it was the flight of the Spaniards. "They fired one far-off and terrific volley into space, and then, before its sound had died away, no less than 10,000 of them, or nearly a third of Cuesta's entire force, betook themselves to flight. The infantry flung away their muskets, the gunners cut their traces and galloped off on their horses: baggage-carts and ammunition waggons swelled the torrent of fugitives." And behind them all Cuesta, in his carriage drawn by nine mules, followed hard. All that day the battle lasted. Towards midnight the firing died away, but only to be renewed on the morrow. Right through the day the battle raged, until, when night again fell, Wellesley stood victorious on the battlefield of Talavera, though 6000 of his men lay dead or dying around him. The loss of those brave lives was not in vain.

"The battle of Talavera," says one, "restored to the successors of Marlborough the glory which for a whole age seemed to have passed from them."

The defeat of his army made Napoleon change his mind about the bravery of British troops and the ability of British commanders.

"It seems this is a man indeed, this Wellesley," said Napoleon when the news reached him at Vienna.

In this the whole world agreed with him. England showered honours on her hero. He was made a peer, with the titles of Baron Douro of Wellesley and Viscount Wellington of Talavera.

Henceforth the "ugly boy Arthur" is known to history as the Duke of Wellington. This is he—

"Who never sold the Truth to serve the hour,
Nor palter'd with Eternal God for power;
Whose life was work, whose language rife
With rugged maxims hewn from life;
Who never spoke against a foe."

35

The Peasant Hero of the Tyrol

"The land we from our fathers had in trust,
And to our children will transmit or die."
—WORDSWORTH (Tyrolese).

From the pursuit of Sir John Moore, Napoleon was hastening to Austria, where a storm was gathering which threatened to be even more serious, than that which had already burst over Spain. To help in the conquest of Spain, Napoleon had removed numbers of French troops from Austria. This therefore was the moment, for that unhappy country to rise, and struggle from under the yoke of France. Nowhere was the appeal to arms answered quicker, than amid the mountains of the Tyrol. The Tyrol was a rugged country, which had belonged to Austria for 400 years, till Napoleon had taken it away and given it to Bavaria. The people might in name belong to Bavaria, but the Tyrolese hearts were faithful to Austria, for which country they were ready to do and to die.

One day in March 1809, the mountaineers were stirred by a proclamation from the Emperor of Austria.

"To arms! to arms! Tyrolese," it ran. "The hour of deliverance is at hand. Now is the time to draw your swords while Napoleon is away. Be faithful to Austria. Young and old, to arms for your Emperor and your country, for your children and your liberty!"

It was received with shouts of joy. They would cast off the yoke of Bavaria and belong to Austria once more, and the ever-growing power of Napoleon should be crushed. At their head was Andrew Hofer, a village innkeeper in the Tyrol. He was a very Hercules for strength, a tall, middle-aged man, wearing always the peasant dress of his country—a large black hat with its broad brim, black ribbons, and a curling feather; a short green coat and red waistcoat, over which he wore green braces; short black breeches and red stockings. To him the faithful peasants looked for guidance, and he did not fail them.

So that the rising should be secret and spontaneous, it was arranged that the signal should be made by throwing sawdust into the river Inn, which would float rapidly down and be understood by the peasants. Success depended on secrecy for Bavarians were at the capital of the Tyrol, Innspruck.

It was the 8th of April, that sawdust was seen to be floating on the river. Throwing off his broad-brimmed hat, Hofer shouted, "Tyrolese, the hour of deliverance is at hand!"

All through the night, the passes of the Engadine seemed alive with moving troops; the stillness was broken by the heavy tread of armed men and the rattling of waggons and guns. Fires blazed from the mountain-tops, and the Tyrol was known to be in open rebellion. A few days later, the main body, numbering some 15,000, had collected on the heights above Innspruck.

"Down with the Bavarians! Long live our Emperor!" cried the peasants, as they rushed to the attack.

After two hours' fighting, they had won their capital back from the Bavarians.

"Your efforts have touched my heart," wrote the Austrian Emperor. "I count you among the most faithful subjects in the Austrian dominions."

In a few days, Bavarian rule was destroyed, and by the end of the month no foreign soldier remained on Tyrolese soil. Many were the brave deeds done by the men and women of the Tyrol to free their country. During one of the conflicts, a young peasant woman came out from a farmhouse, with a cask of beer on her head for her fighting countrymen. Heedless of the enemy's fire she made her way to the scene of action, when a bullet struck the cask. Undaunted, she placed her thumb in the hole made by the bullet, and gave the weary peasants a drink in spite of the danger she was in.

Meanwhile Napoleon had reached Austria. On the morning of July 16, the two largest armies that had ever been brought face to face in Europe, met to fight. The great world-conqueror gained a complete victory over the Austrians at Wagram, entered Vienna once more in triumph, and dictated his own terms to rebellious Austria.

This was a terrible blow to the peasants of the Tyrol. Austria might make peace with Napoleon, but the men of the Tyrol determined to go on fighting under Andrew Hofer. In vain did the Emperor beg them to lay down their arms, and not prolong a conflict that was over and throw away their lives; in vain was Andrew Hofer bidden to appear before the Bavarians, who had retaken Innspruck.

"I will do so," was the obstinate answer; "but it shall be at the head of ten thousand men."

At the head of his peasant patriots, he once more posted his army on the heights above Innspruck. Below lay a road, along which the Bavarians must pass. Suddenly a cry rang out "For Tyrol strike!" and huge stones, trunks of trees, and stones were hurled down pitilessly on the heads of the bewildered

Bavarians passing below. The destruction was complete; and on Napoleon's birthday, August 15, Hofer triumphantly entered his capital. He took up his abode in the imperial castle, and carried on the government in the name of the Emperor.

Then came another letter from the Emperor saying decidedly, "I have been obliged to make peace with France." This meant that the Tyrol had been given back to Bavaria. Then, at last, the Tyrolese threw down their arms and lost heart. Hofer hid himself in a lonely little Alpine hut with his wife and children, and here, one bitter January day, he was found by French soldiers, who marched him through the deep snow to his trial as a traitor. The trial was short, the verdict certain. He was to be shot in twenty-four hours, before the Austrians could hear of his capture. Bravely Hofer had fought, bravely he died. Arrived at the place of execution, the French guards formed a square around the peasant hero. A drummer boy stepped forward and offered to bind his eyes, and bade him kneel.

"No," cried Hofer firmly; "I am used to stand upright before my Creator, and in that posture will I deliver up my spirit to him."

Firmly he uttered the word "Fire!" Firmly he died.

Twenty years later, the Tyrol was restored to Austria, and in the cathedral church the Austrians erected a statue in white Tyrolese marble to the peasant, who had fought and died for his country.

36

The Empire at its Height

"I have touch'd the highest point of all my greatness."
—SHAKSPERE

Having made peace with Austria and suppressed the restless Tyrol, Napoleon returned to Paris. His great ambition was still unsatisfied, and he now made up his mind to take a further step to improve his wonderful position.

"I and my house," he said grandly to his French subjects, "will ever be found ready to sacrifice everything, even our dearest ties and feelings, to the welfare of the French people."

This was the first time he had hinted to the world, of the great step he was about to take, in divorcing his faithful wife Josephine, in order to marry a royal princess of Europe. Josephine, the widow of a French general, had married Napoleon in the days when he was a lonely young Corsican, making his way upwards in Paris. She and her two children had been loved by him for fourteen years. To her son, Eugene, Napoleon had given important posts; her daughter, Hortense, had been married to Louis Bonaparte, and was now Queen of Holland. Josephine had shared Napoleon's humble fortunes; she had been crowned Empress of the French but six years before.

One November evening, in the palace of the Tuileries, where they lived, Napoleon told Josephine of the step he intended to take. It was for the good of the empire, he told her. Was she willing to make this sacrifice?

It was a scene that left its mark on the stern Emperor. Josephine pleaded and entreated until, quite overcome, she fell fainting at his feet. Tenderly he raised her and carried her down the narrow staircase leading to her room. But Josephine had received a wound past healing, and she disappears from history—a heart-broken woman.

Napoleon now turned to Russia to ask the hand of Alexander's sister, but this was refused him. He then turned to Austria, and was accepted by the Emperor Francis, for his daughter Maria Louisa, who was just eighteen. Her journey from Vienna to the French capital is not unlike that of her great-aunt Marie Antoinette forty years before, as she drove with her Austrian ladies to meet the bridegroom, she had never yet seen. Napoleon rode forth to meet her, and they were married with great splendour in Paris.

Napoleon was now at the height of his greatness and glory. He had extended the French Empire far and wide. The rich lands beyond the Rhine owned his sway, in the person of his youngest brother Jerome. His brother Louis, having abdicated the throne of Holland, that country had just been formally annexed to France. The Pope had been carried captive to France, and the Papal States now belonged to the French Empire. Paris, Rome, and Amsterdam were the three great capitals of the world-empire. Sweden was not strong enough to resist his power, Austria was at peace. For the throne of restless Spain, Joseph Bonaparte was still contending, but Napoleon had no fears in that quarter. As yet Russia was following his lead, but it was evident she was fast "slipping out of the leading-strings of Tilsit."

When Alexander of Russia had heard of Napoleon's marriage with Maria Louisa, he had exclaimed, "The next thing will be to drive us back into our forests."

He was not far wrong. Russia had not been active enough in closing her northern ports to British trade. To press yet closer this "Continental system," as it was called, was Napoleon's only hope of still crushing England. If Alexander would not submit, Alexander must be made to submit.

Napoleon was feeling more secure than ever just now. A son had been born to him in March 1811, and he had presented the baby Napoleon to his people, as King of Rome. For this child of the great empire was reserved the saddest of fates.

"Now begins the finest epoch of my reign,'' the Emperor had cried in his joy, at the birth of a son.

He did not know, that it was the moment of his decline.

It was August 16—the day after his birthday when the little Napoleon was six months old—that Napoleon sketched to his ministry his whole plan of the great Russian campaign, which had long been occupying his mind. He was going to invade Russia with an overwhelming force, and compel her to close every port to English ships. Now was the time to strike, for the Peninsular war was at its height, and England was already at war with the United States.

A tremendous force was collected, numbering 600,000 men. There were Austrians, Italians, Poles, Prussians, as well as French—all the soldiers of the empire. There were crowned heads in command, and tried generals. Such a host had never been seen before in modern history.

On May 16, 1812, Napoleon himself arrived at Dresden, with his wife Maria Louisa and the little child-king of Rome. Here the Emperor of Austria came to meet them, and various crowned heads paid court to the man who, for the last time, was figuring as the "king of kings."

A fortnight later, he was on his way to Russia at the head of his Grand Army. Arrived at the banks of the Niemen—the river forming the boundary between Russia and Prussia—Napoleon stopped. He was not very far from Tilsit, where he had made peace with Alexander on the raft in this same river. Would it be peace again with the Tsar or war? He issued a proclamation to his soldiers.

"Soldiers," it ran, "Russia is dragged on by her fate: her destiny must be fulfilled. Let us march, let us cross the Niemen; let us carry war into her territories."

In a very different spirit Alexander was addressing his troops on the farther side.

"Soldiers," he was saying, "you fight for your native land. Your Emperor is amongst you. God fights against the aggressor."

Alexander spoke truly when he said, "I have learnt to know him now. Napoleon or I: I or Napoleon: we cannot reign side by side."

37

The Shannon and the Chesapeake

"Old England's sons are English yet, old England's hearts are strong,
And still she wears her coronet aflame with sword and song.
As in their pride our fathers died, if need be, so die we;
So wield we still, gainsay who will, the sceptre of the sea."
—MERIVALE.

Napoleon had closed all European ports against British commerce. But as the fleet of Great Britain was supreme upon the seas, she made answer that henceforth no colonial goods should be obtainable in France except through British ships. The United States of America, as a new nation, taking neither the side of England, nor, of France in their terrific struggle, resented this action, for it stopped their direct trading with France. Indeed it paralysed all trade, and in June 1812 the United States declared war on Great Britain.

It was a bold challenge. England indeed had her hands full with Napoleon in Europe; but even now her triumph was beginning. Napoleon was already on his fatal march to Moscow; Wellington had seized the two frontier fortresses of Ciudad Rodrigo and Badajoz. But England had the greatest navy in the world—a thousand sail; and the United States had the smallest—about twenty ships. The young Republic was full of confidence in their newly found strength; they had lost the guiding hand of Washington, who always upheld peace with the mother country.

It was somewhat natural to find that England, rich in her traditions of Nelson and Trafalgar, thought but little of this challenge, until one day the startling news reached her, that five of her ships of war had been captured by the United States. Something must be done at once, to wipe out this unlooked-for disgrace, that had fallen on the British flag.

One strong unassuming English sailor now took the matter into his own hands. Captain Broke, of H.M.S. Shannon, had spent the winter off Halifax, Nova Scotia, where he heard of the declaration of war between the two countries. He at once began to drill his gunners more severely than ever, until he made every one of them a good shot. The discipline on board his ship was splendid. His crew had worked with him for the last seven years; they had shared hardships and dangers together; and there was complete understanding between master and man. All were alike burning with desire to meet the ships of the United States. The Shannon herself was not a large ship. She carried thirty-eight guns and 284 men. She bore the marks of her service in the icy regions of the north. "Her sides were rusty, her sails were weather-soiled; a solitary flag flew from her mizzen-peak, and even its blue had become bleached by sun and rain and wind to a dingy grey."

In May 1813 the Shannon lay off Boston. Captain Broke determined to end the naval dispute by a single challenge of ship to ship. As antagonist he chose the Chesapeake, a ship larger than the Shannon, and carrying more men. On Tuesday, June 1, he despatched a letter to Captain Lawrence of the Chesapeake, which had been lying for months past in Boston Harbour.

"As the Chesapeake appears now ready for sea," ran the challenge, "I request that you will do me the favour to meet the Shannon with her, ship to ship, to try the fortune of our respective flags. Choose your terms and place, and let us meet."

Captain Lawrence was a formidable foe. He had already captured the Peacock, an English battleship, and was known to be one of the most gallant of men.

Having sent the challenge, Captain Broke now went up to the mast-head of the Shannon and watched anxiously for any movement on the part of the hostile ship. A faint breeze rippled over the waters of the Boston Harbour, while the summer sun lit up the town beyond. Mid-day came, and Broke descended to the deck.

"She will surely be out to-day or to-morrow," he said, pointing over the gleaming waters. The hours passed on. Daylight was beginning to wane, when a cry rang out through the ship, "She is coming!"

It was true. Sail after sail spread forth, flag after flag unfurled, and with all speed the Chesapeake was seen bearing down on her expectant foe, attended by barges and pleasure-boats.

To the men of Boston, it seemed that Lawrence sailed forth to certain victory. They crowded house-tops and hills to see his success; they prepared a banquet to celebrate his triumphant return.

Slowly and in grim silence the Shannon and Chesapeake drew near. On board the Shannon, Broke was addressing his men.

"Shannons!" he cried, "the Americans have lately triumphed over the British flag; they have said that England had forgotten how to fight. You will let them see to-day, there are Englishmen in the Shannon who still know how to fight. Don't cheer. Go quietly to your posts. I know you will all do your duty."

As the Chesapeake moved on, a blaze of fluttering colours, one sailor looked sadly at the one faded blue flag above him.

"Mayn't we have three ensigns, sir, like she has?" he asked.

"No," answered the Captain; "we have always been an unassuming ship."

The fight soon began. Never was there a braver, shorter, or more deadly conflict. On both sides the fire was tremendous, but the well-trained British gunners on the Shannon fired with deadly aim; every shot told. The rigging of the Chesapeake was torn, her stern was beaten in, her decks were swept by fire. For six minutes the conflict raged. Lawrence had already fallen, mortally wounded. As the two ships ground together, Broke shouted above the din, "Follow me who can!" Then bounding on to the deck of the Chesapeake, over the bodies of dead and dying, the English sailors boarded the American ship, and thirteen minutes after the first shot had been fired, the British flag waved over the Chesapeake.

"Blow her up! blow her up!" cried the dying Lawrence.

But it was too late. The foe had yielded; resistance was over. Broke, now lying badly wounded, had won. He had restored confidence in his country's fleet, but at tremendous cost. 252 men from the two ships fell that day. It was characteristic of the Captain of the Shannon, that he should enter in his journal for that day only two words—"Took Chesapeake."

This ended the naval war, though fighting by land went on between the two countries till 1814, when peace was made, which has never been broken since.

38

Napoleon's Retreat from Moscow

"No pitying voice commands a halt,
No courage can dispel the dire assault:
Distracted, spiritless, benumbed, and blind,
Whole legions sink—and in one instant find
Burial and death."
—WORDSWORTH.

The story of Napoleon's advance to and retreat from Moscow, is one of the most pathetic in human history. Full of spirit, the Grand Army had started, but already difficulties were beginning. It took three days to cross the Niemen, by means of pontoon bridges thrown across; but they reached the far side unmolested, and pursued their way over the sandy wastes. The solitude of the way, the sultry heat of a Russian midsummer, and drenching thunderstorms depressed the spirits of the army. By the time they reached Vilna—some seventy miles on—10,000 horses had perished, 30,000 stragglers had deserted, and there were 25,000 sick men, and the transports as yet ever so far behind.

It was not till July 16, that an advance was possible, and the Grand Army could once more march on its way to Moscow. Fever and disease now played their part, and food ran short. No human genius could have achieved the stupendous task, Napoleon had now undertaken. So fearful was the prospect, that Napoleon seriously thought of putting off the invasion till the spring. But the temptation of conquest was strong upon him, and once more the great host moved forward to Smolensko. The Russians moved out of each city as the French advanced.

At last, on September 7, the two armies met some seventy miles from Moscow, and a tremendous battle was fought at Borodino. Both sides claimed the victory, which neither had won, though 40,000 French and 30,000 Russians lay wounded or dead on the battlefield.

The Grand Army, now so reduced in size, reached Moscow a week later. There lay the famous city at last at the foot of the hill, with its gardens, its churches, its river, its steeples crowned with golden balls, all flashing and blazing in the bright morning sunlight of that autumn day.

"Moscow! Moscow!" cried the delighted soldiers.

"Yes, here at last is the famous city," said Napoleon, reining in his horse.

The conqueror entered his new capital, expecting to be met with the keys of the city and the submission of Alexander. What was his surprise, then, to find the city empty and deserted! The houses were closed, the streets were bare. To add to this disappointment, flames were soon seen bursting forth from various quarters. The Russians had set their capital on fire!

For three days and nights the fire raged furiously, till from the very Kremlin or citadel, where Napoleon was staying, flames issued forth. A great part of the wonderful city was destroyed, and the question of food-supply again faced Napoleon. The Russians had swept the district bare.

Still Napoleon hoped to bring Alexander to terms, but the Tsar's proclamation to his people showed, that he understood the peril of the French in Moscow: "The enemy is in deserted Moscow, without means of existence. He has the wreck of his army in Moscow. He is in the heart of Russia, without a single Russian at his feet, while our forces are increasing round him. To escape famine, he must pass through the close ranks of our brave soldiers."

Still Napoleon lingered on. September passed, October had begun. The idea of spending a winter in the blackened city, with only salted horse-flesh to eat, was intolerable, and at last the order to retreat was given.

It was the 18th of October, just a month after their entry into the capital, that the French army once more filed through the gates. There were about 100,000 fighting men now, with a number of sick. Besides these, were a number of followers, stragglers, prisoners, baggage-bearers,—men of all nations, speaking all languages,—one idea of escaping the terrors of a Russian winter hurrying them onwards. So far the weather was fine. A few days after their start, a Russian army blocked their way. A battle was fought, and the Grand Army was further reduced to 65,000 men. On they hastened. They could rest and get food at Smolensko, if only they could reach it, before the snow began. On November 6, winter suddenly came upon them. The clear blue sky disappeared, the sun was seen no more, bitter blasts of wind cut through them; and then came thick flakes of snow, darkening the whole air. Through whirlwinds of snow and sleet, the troops forced their dreary way. Their clothes froze on them, icicles hung from their beards. Those who sank down from very weariness, rose no more. All order was at an end. Muskets fell from the frozen hands that carried them. Before, above, around them, was nothing but snow. Now and again they tried to light fires to thaw their clothes and cook their wretched meal of horse-flesh.

"Smolensko, Smolensko," they murmured to one another.

It was November 14, before they reached this longed-for goal and literally fought for food. Two-thirds of the army had perished in twenty-five days, and much was yet before them. They must push on quickly,—push on through bands of attacking Russians all the way. The firmness of Napoleon never left him. In the midst of the wildest swamp, in snowstorms and darkness, by night and day, he never lost sight of the fact, that this handful of hungry, frost-bitten men was the Grand Army of France, and that he, their leader, was the conqueror of Europe. They were now within three days march of the river Beresina, which had to be crossed, when news arrived, that the Russians had broken down the bridge. The Emperor struck the ground with his stick, and, raising his eyes to heaven, cried, "Is it written there that henceforth every step shall be a fault?"

The situation was indeed desperate. They must march on and cross the river under fire, and across bridges of their own making. In the midst of their sufferings, they never doubted their Emperor. His genius had always triumphed; he would lead them to victory yet. On they dragged—on towards the fatal Beresina. It was November 25, and late that evening, the first pile was driven into the muddy bank of the river for the bridge. All night they worked, up to their necks in water, struggling with pieces of ice carried down by the stream. The lights from the Russian fires gleamed from the opposite side. One after another his generals tried to persuade Napoleon to escape, but he refused to desert his army in the face of so great danger.

All went well for a time. Napoleon and some 2000 soldiers were across, and the bridge was heavily weighted with masses of struggling men, when with a thundering crash and a cry of horror the bridge broke in the middle. The Russians now rushed to the attack, and terrible indeed was the onslaught. Thousands were drowned, thousands were killed. The scene was terrible. On November 29, Napoleon and the remains of the Grand Army pushed on towards Vilna, where they arrived after a fearful march through ice and snow. Here at last the Emperor left them, to push on to Paris as fast as he might.

Then, and not till then, the Grand Army lost heart. The weather grew worse; the very birds froze in the air and dropped dead at their feet. On they tramped, with their eyes cast down. To stop meant certain death. The only sound in the stillness, was the dull tread of their own feet in the snow and the feeble groans of the dying. Their only food was boiled horse-flesh, together with a little rye meal, kneaded into muffins with snow-water, and seasoned with the powder of their cartridges.

Out of the 600,000 men who had so proudly crossed the river Niemen seven months before, for the conquest of Russia, only 20,000 staggered across the frozen river. The rest of that mighty host "lay at rest under Nature's winding-sheet of snow."

Just a week before Christmas, Napoleon reached the Tuileries.

"All had gone well," he said. "Moscow was in his power; but the cold of the winter had caused a general calamity, by reason of which the army had sustained very great losses."

39

Wellington's Victories in Spain

"For this is England's greatest son,
He that gain'd a hundred fights,
Nor ever lost an English gun."
—TENNYSON (Wellington).

While Napoleon was marching on his ill-fated expedition to Russia, Wellington was wresting Spain from the grip of France. The hardly won victory of Talavera had not been much use, and the English had been obliged to fall back on Portugal in face of the huge French armies, which threatened them on all sides. The winter of 1810 was spent by Wellington, in securing Lisbon against the vast armies of Napoleon.

To the north of the capital, run two rugged lines of mountains stretching from the coast, washed by the Atlantic Ocean, to the mouth of the river Tagus. No less than 7000 Portuguese peasants were set to work, to build forts and construct earthworks, to turn these mountains into natural defences for Lisbon. Bristling with guns, these famous Lines of Torres Vedras, as they are called, formed a formidable barrier. The summer of 1810 found Marshal Massena, of Wagram fame, in command of the French army destined by Napoleon for the conquest of Portugal. In the ranks were 70,000 hero veterans of Marengo and Austerlitz.

"We will drive the English into the sea," they said with confidence, as they took fort after fort on their triumphant march.

Wellington awaited them on the heights of Busaco, thus barring the road to Lisbon.

"There are certainly many bad roads in Portugal, but the enemy has taken decidedly the worst," said Wellington.

From their high perch, the English could see Massena's great host marching onwards, their bayonets gleaming, their helmets sparkling in the valley below. It was still cold grey dawn on the morning of September 29, when the splendid French troops swept bravely up the steep face of the hill of Busaco. The English grimly awaited them at the top. Neither side was wanting in courage. But it was only a few minutes, before the unhappy heroes of Austerlitz were rolling down the steep face of Busaco, the slopes of which were soon thick with dead and dying.

Massena now heard for the first time of the Lines of Torres Vedras, that tremendous barrier, which made it impossible for him to reach Lisbon. He had been warned of Wellington's work, but not of the existence of the hills.

"Yes, yes," he said angrily, as the truth dawned on him, "Wellington built the works, but he did not make the mountains."

For six weeks he camped hopelessly before the Lines, his army wasting with disease and starvation. Not till 30,000 soldiers had perished did he retreat, leaving Wellington triumphant behind his lines. The bitter winter passed; spring gave way to summer, summer to autumn, and still the conflict in Portugal raged on. It was not till the winter of 1812, that Wellington was able to turn his attention to Spain. His way was barred by the two great frontier fortresses of Ciudad Rodrigo and Badajoz, to the north and south of the river Tagus. Secretly and hastily, Wellington laid his plans to besiege the most northerly of these, Ciudad Rodrigo. It was strongly defended by the French, but the English smote it with strokes so furious and with such "breathless speed" that it fell in twelve days. It was midwinter; the rivers were edged with ice, snow lay on the ground, bitter blasts blew over the ramparts, the nights were black dark, but Wellington was undaunted.

The siege began on January 8. It ended on the 19th with a tremendous assault. Up the black face of the grim fortress swarmed the English in the dark night. Racing over broken stones, scrambling over huge rocks, upwards they rushed till the summit was gained and the French garrison driven back.

"It was the rush of the English stormers up the breaches of Ciudad Rodrigo, that began the fall of the French Empire."

Leaving a Spanish garrison in possession of the fortress, Wellington now with "heroic madness" pushed on for the next attack. Badajoz stood on a rocky ridge of extraordinary strength. Twice the English had already tried to take it: twice they had failed. But Wellington was "strong in his own warlike genius, and in the quality of the troops he commanded."

On the stormy night of March 17 the siege began. On April 6 an assault was ordered. At 10 o'clock on that still dark night the English troops stood firm and ready for the attack. No less than five assaults were to be made at different points: each was equally heroic in its mad rush to the top under fire. But hour after hour of that terrible night passed away, and still the stormers had not taken Badajoz.

"Why do you not come into Badajoz," cried the French from the top, to the English below, who gazed upwards at the grim height bristling with French guns, unable to advance, refusing to retreat. Wellington watched, his face grey with anxiety, for the cost in human life was tremendous. It was not till daylight, that the men gained the heights, and the French commander, who had been badly wounded, surrendered. In that wild night-fight Wellington had lost heavily; and as he gazed on the slope, strewn with the dead bodies of his soldiers, he burst into tears.

40

Spain for the Spaniards

"Not stirring words, nor gallant deeds alone,—
Plain patient work fulfilled that length of life;
Duty, not glory—service, not a throne,
Inspired his effort, set for him the strife."
—CLOUGH (Wellington).

Much had been done by Wellington, in the capture of these two strongholds, but much yet remained to do. Spain must be wrested from the grip of the French, and he must fulfil his commands.

While Napoleon and his Grand Army were starting on their fatal march to Moscow, Wellington was already advancing into Spain. On July 22 he met the French army at Salamanca, a very old hill-city, famous in the days of Hannibal 222 years B.C. This battle has been summed up by a Frenchman as the "battle in which 40,000 men were beaten in forty minutes." Wellington himself considered it one of his greatest victories. Let us watch him during the day of battle. Shortly after mid-day he entered a farmyard, where food was prepared for him. Stumping about and munching his food, Wellington was constantly looking at the French army, where important movements were taking place. Suddenly mounting in haste, he galloped to a spot of observation. Closing his spy-glass with a snap, he said to the Spaniard at his side, "My dear Alava, the French are lost."

The French Marshal had made a serious blunder. Wellington saw his chance had come.

"Ned," he cried to his brother-in-law in command of some troops, "d'ye see those fellows on the hill? At them, and drive them to the devil." Then to his nephew, afterwards the famous Lord Raglan, he said, "Watch the French through your glass: I am going to take a rest. When they reach that copse near the gap in the hills, wake me."

He lay down in his cloak on the heath, among the sweet gum-cistus flowers, and was soon fast asleep.

Between three and four, they wakened him as he had ordered. Before it was dusk, the French army was defeated. Through the moonlight Wellington pressed after the flying foe. The victory was complete: the way to Madrid was clear. Just a month before Napoleon entered Moscow, Wellington entered

Madrid. The Spaniards in the capital threw themselves weeping at his feet, hailing him as their deliverer from the French.

But Spain was not yet delivered from the French. Large armies and tried generals from France still threatened the English, and Wellington had to leave Madrid. England was complaining bitterly of her general. For five years he had been fighting, and it seemed as if the French gripped Spain as tightly as ever. Money and precious lives had been sacrificed. Napoleon would soon return victorious from Russia, and all chance of saving Spain would be at an end.

Wellington spent the winter in Portugal preparing for a final overthrow of the French. Joseph Bonaparte was now in command, having quarrelled with his brother's marshals.

And so, when the vines began to shoot and the wheat was ankle deep, British drums and bugles sounded a long farewell to Portugal, for this must be the last campaign in the Peninsula. It is said when Wellington, at the head of his well-trained army, crossed the Douro into Spain, he turned round on his horse, and, taking off his hat, cried, "Farewell, Portugal: I shall never see you again!"

Then on he marched, his iron will more determined than ever, on towards the Pyrenees to cut off Joseph, who had left Madrid for the last time, in his brief and troubled reign.

"I looked beyond the limits of Spain," said Wellington as he marched on. "I knew the impression my advance would make on Europe."

Joseph's army now filled the valley of Vittoria—70,000 strong. He still might escape over the Pyrenees back to France. But Wellington took care to block the royal road to France.

At dawn on the morning of June 22, the battle of Vittoria began. By evening, the unfortunate King Joseph was flying from the field, and Wellington, standing victorious on the scene of action, was watching the retreating French. As far as the eye could reach, fields and hillsides were covered with a flying multitude of soldiers and camp-followers. The streets of Vittoria were blocked with waggons and carriages. The rout was complete: the splendid French army was shattered.

The spoil that fell to Wellington was enormous. It was the result of five years' plunder in Spain. Chests of money, baggage, gunpowder, plate, pictures, were left behind. A general rush took place to seize the forsaken treasure, and soon the plain was strewn with things; while the soldiers, that night, marched about the camp arrayed in turbans and plumes, carrying about French monkeys, lap-dogs, and parrots.

When Napoleon heard of the disaster, he was furious.

"What is going on in Spain?" he cried. "Joseph could have collected a hundred thousand men: they might have beaten the whole of England."

"Tell Joseph," he added later, "his behaviour has never ceased to bring misfortune on my army for the last five years. It is time to make an end of it. There was a world of folly in the whole business."

No wonder poor Joseph vanished from history. He sailed away to America, where he ended his days in peace. Once he was offered the crown of Mexico.

"I have worn two crowns: I will not risk a third," he answered pathetically.

So after five years of dogged perseverance Wellington stood on the summit of the Pyrenees—a conqueror.

Napoleon at last had found a rival.

41

The Fall of the Empire

"Farewell to the land where the gloom of my glory
Arose and o'ershadowed the earth with her name;
She abandons me now, but the page of her story,
The brightest or blackest, is filled with my fame."
—BYRON (Napoleon's Farewell).

Napoleon had returned to Paris at Christmas-time in 1812. The following spring found him taking the field again, for Prussia had suddenly sprung to arms and allied herself with Russia against France.

Napoleon had lost his Grand Army. The heroes of that fatal march, slept their last sleep beneath the winter snows of Russia, but he was undaunted still. His veterans were dead, but he called on the youth of the French empire. He commandeered lads of seventeen—the last hopes of France—to fight his battles. They were not soldiers, but children; enthusiastic, superbly brave, but without the strength or endurance needed for such a campaign. And it sounds almost brutal to hear their general complaining, that they "choked his hospitals with their sick and strewed his roads with their dead bodies."

"I grew up in the field, and a man like me troubles himself little about the lives of a million of men," Napoleon had explained.

And so great was his genius, that with this young army, he defeated the Russians and Prussians in the two battles fought at Lutzen and Bautzen.

The defeated armies now looked to Austria for help, and not in vain. Austria joined them, England joined them. One by one the nations of Europe arose, to shake off the yoke of Napoleon.

"A year ago," said the French Emperor, "all Europe marched with us; now it all marches against us."

It was five months after he had received the news of Wellington's victory at Vittoria, that Napoleon was beaten at last by the allies at Leipzig, in Germany. It was a terrible fight, lasting three days, and known to history as the "Battle of the Nations." It was almost a massacre in its loss of life; but it shook Napoleon's throne, and it broke his power.

On November 9, 1813, Napoleon returned unexpectedly to Paris. He found the capital sullen and gloomy at the news of fresh disaster to the Empire. His Empress threw herself into his arms in floods of tears. The country was crying for peace.

"Inspire my papa, O God, with the desire to make peace, for the welfare of France and of us all," was the nightly prayer of the baby-king of Rome.

Napoleon listened and smiled. But he rejected the terms of peace now offered by the four allies, and they prepared for the invasion of France herself.

"We must march to Paris," said the famous Prussian general, Blücher. "Napoleon has paid his visit to every capital in Europe, and we can do no less than return the compliment."

Yet once again, Napoleon prepared to march against them. On January 23, he held his last great reception in the palace of the Tuileries.

"Gentlemen," he said to the assembled company, "a part of France is invaded. I am about to place myself at the head of my army, and with the help of God and the valour of my troops I hope to drive the enemy back beyond the frontiers."

Then he led forward his Empress and the little king of Rome, a flaxen-haired child of three, dressed in the uniform of the National Guard.

"If," he added in a broken voice—"If the enemy approaches the capital, I intrust all that I hold dearest in the world—my wife and my son—to the devotion of the National Guard."

Amid sobs and shouts of fidelity, he carried round the child in his arms. Before the morning dawned on January 25, he said good-bye to Maria Louisa and his little son, neither of whom he ever saw again.

He now placed himself at the head of his hastily formed army, which was to oppose the great hosts of soldiers pouring down upon him from beyond the Rhine. A nine weeks' campaign followed. Napoleon was as full of genius and resource as ever, but the Powers arrayed against him were too strong for his boy army. Slowly he was pushed back from the Rhine to the boundaries of France. Toward the end of March, the Allies were nearing Paris. Still Napoleon did not despair. With a magnificent courage, he led on his weary troops.

"If the enemy reaches Paris, the Empire is no more," he exclaimed, as he pushed vigorously forward.

On March 30 Maria Louisa and her little son had fled from the doomed city. Napoleon was even now within ten miles: he might yet be in time to save the town. Forward—forward to Paris. Then they told him the news. "Sire, it is too late: Paris has capitulated."

Slowly the truth burnt into the brain of the fallen and defeated Emperor. Paris was his no longer. He could see the enemy's watch-fires glowing against the northern sky; he knew the heights of the city were bristling with cannon which forbade approach. His great courage gave way at last.

Meanwhile Alexander of Russia and Frederick William of Prussia were riding side by side through Paris, while the people shouted for the restoration of Louis XVIII. as their king. Nothing was left for the Emperor of the French save to abdicate.

"The allied Powers having proclaimed that the Emperor Napoleon was the sole obstacle to the re-establishment of peace in Europe, faithful to his oaths, he declares that he renounces for himself and his heirs, the thrones of France and Italy, and that there is no sacrifice, not even that of life, which he is not ready to make for the interest of France." So ran the words whereby Napoleon signed away his mighty empire.

"Obtain the best terms you can for France. For myself I ask nothing," he said gloomily to the messenger between himself and the Allies.

Yet his anguish was great when he found that his great empire was to be exchanged for the little island of Elba away in the Mediterranean, between Corsica and the coast of Italy. Such a position seemed intolerable. He sought to take his own life, but failed.

"Fate has decreed," he exclaimed; "I must live and await all that Providence has in store for me."

Preparations went forward.

"It is all like a dream," he said one day, putting his hand wearily to his head.

On April 20 he said good-bye to the Imperial Guard, drawn up before him. Tears fell from his eyes, as he dismounted in their midst.

"All Europe," he said, "has armed against me. France herself has deserted me. Be faithful to the new king whom your country has chosen. Do not lament my fate. I could have died. I shall write with my pen of the deeds we have done together. Bring hither the eagle. Beloved eagle! may the kisses I bestow on you long resound in the hearts of the brave. Farewell, my children; farewell, my brave companions,—farewell!"

Then, kissing the war-stained banner of France, he turned from them and went on his way, while the sobs of the men, who had fought for him, fell on his ear.

He was accompanied to Elba, his new home, by four representatives of Russia, Prussia, Austria, and England. Maria Louisa was safe in her father's keeping, and now refused to follow her husband into exile. Alone, bereft of all his friends, forsaken by wife and child, the fallen Emperor arrived at his island home.

"It must be confessed," he said smiling, as he stood one day at the top of the highest hill in Elba,—"It must be confessed, that my island is very small."

42

Story of the Steam-engine

"Science moves, but slowly, slowly, creeping on from point to point."
—TENNYSON

To imagine a world without trains on the land and steamers on the sea is, in these days, very difficult. And yet, through the times of Nelson and Napoleon, neither of these were available for transit. It was not till early in the nineteenth century, that the first steamer crossed the ocean, or the first train steamed along its iron rails with passengers.

All through the long ages of the past, men had been groping after the idea, that steam might be made to move heavy weights. But how? Point by point, step by step, they gradually discovered the great power of steam. Men, whose names were never written in the world's great history, struggled after nature's secret, each adding some atom of knowledge, to help those that came after.

Thus the express train, that to-day can cover fifty miles an hour, and the great ocean steamer, with its possible speed of twenty miles an hour, were not the invention of any one man or any one nation.

An ancient Greek at Alexandria, in the olden days, made the first steam-engine. It was only a toy, but it showed the power of steam to turn a ball suspended over a boiling caldron of water. But the years rolled on after this, and little was done till the art of printing, made known to the world, the discoveries of the men of old, and the increased industry of Europe, demanded some better means of transit for goods.

Throughout the seventeenth century, Italians, Dutch, French, and English worked at this magic power of steam. Through success and failure they laboured on. But the eighteenth century dawned to find, that they had not got further than erecting clumsy engines at the mouths of mines, to raise water.

It would take too long to tell of the accidents, that befell some of the new inventions. There was the poor Frenchman Papin, who, after a hard life and much valuable invention, made a steamship. It was merely a boat, into which he put a pumping-engine, which turned a water-wheel, which in its turn moved a paddle-wheel, and so moved the boat onwards down the river. But the boatmen on the river feared this new mode of steaming: they thought it would destroy their work; and one night they destroyed the poor little steamship, leaving its owner and inventor to flee for his life.

There was the man who made an engine on four iron legs, to move like a horse; but it didn't move like a horse at all. There was the steam-engine, from which great things were expected, that suddenly burst, and it was a wonder that any of the bystanders escaped with their lives.

A great impetus was given to inventors, by the discovery of a young Scotsman—James Watt—towards the middle of the eighteenth century. He had always been greatly attracted by the power of steam, and as a little lad, had made models of useless little steam-engines. One Sunday afternoon, he was walking by himself in a grassy meadow near Glasgow, thinking as usual about his engine, when a new idea came into his head with regard to steam. He set to work to make an engine on this new principle, and all men acknowledged, that a great stride had been made in the world of discovery. Watt's engine worked with great power, and used less coal than any before, but it made a terrible noise, and was very far from perfection.

Meanwhile an American, named Fulton, was working at steamships. Watt's engine supplied a want. He ordered one to be fitted into his ship, and launched the "Clermont" on the river at New York in the year 1807. The boat did 150 miles in thirty-two hours—the first voyage of any considerable length made by a steamer. But she terrified those who saw her. Dry pine-wood was used for fuel, and the flames rose high into the air, while the noise of the machinery and paddles so frightened the boatmen on the river that they threw themselves on their knees to pray for protection from the horrible monster, which was moving on the waters, "breathing flames and smoke, defying wind and tide."

Great Britain and America were now shooting ahead of the other nations with their inventions. It was reserved for an Englishman, to put the first engine on a railroad. In the year 1808, Trevithick built a railroad in London, and set at work a steam-carriage, which he called "Catch-me-who-can." It made a journey of about twelve miles an hour on a circular railway, but one day it was thrown off the track by the breaking of a rail, and never started again.

Still the idea was sound, and a few years later George Stephenson made his first successful engine in the north of England. He called it the "Blücher," after the great Prussian general, who had fought against Napoleon, and was going to fight again in the course of the next year. The Blücher was clumsy and noisy enough, but it succeeded in drawing after it eight loaded carriages of coal, at the rate of four miles an hour, and worked regularly for some time.

It was yet some years later, before passengers were willing to trust themselves behind such engines or on board such steamers, as have been described. The flames, the smoke, the jerky movements, the rattling of machinery, were enough to frighten the most courageous. But the new discoveries were enough to put a new face on the commerce and industries of Great Britain. The iron- and coal-fields of the north were worked with redoubled vigour; lines were laid from the mines to the towns and the coast, and the steam-engine proved to be the most wonderful instrument that human industry ever had at its command. Great Britain had finally achieved, what the whole world had sought for thousands of years, and by this achievement, she rose to be the greatest manufacturing country the world has yet seen.

43

The Congress of Vienna

"All Europe's bound-lines, drawn afresh in blood."
—Mrs BROWNING.

Napoleon's great empire had passed away. His fall restored peace to the troubled nations of Europe, whose boundaries he had destroyed.

A great congress of European kings and statesmen, now met at the Austrian capital, Vienna, to readjust these boundaries and to reinstate kings to their rightful thrones. It was a wondrous meeting. There was the Emperor of Austria himself, with his thin figure and sallow face, the father of Maria Louisa, Empress of the French in name alone; there was the manly form of the Tsar of Russia, Alexander, with his wife, to whom the musician Beethoven had been playing; there was the King of Prussia, tall and very grave; the white-haired King of Denmark; and numerous other great men, including the Duke of Wellington.

Picnics, balls, and banquets were the order of the day. Hundreds of royal carriages, painted in green and silver, rolled through the streets of Vienna, carrying the Emperor's guests from place to place. Outside all these festive scenes sat Maria Louisa. Her father's guests were assembled to undo the work of Napoleon her husband, even now an exile at Elba. Right away from the gay throng, she lived at her palace, her servants still wearing the French liveries of the court of Napoleon, her little son still dressed in the embroidered uniform of a French hussar, playing with his French toys.

Meanwhile the work of the Congress was progressing. Louis XVIII. had been recalled from England—where he had lived since the death of his brother Louis XVI.—to take possession of the throne of France. Ferdinand of Spain returned from exile to rule over his Spanish kingdom once more; the Pope returned to Rome; the Prince of Orange was made King of Holland.

Suddenly, one day, the news rang through Europe that Napoleon had escaped from Elba, and was even now in France. The news took eight days to reach Vienna. The Congress met, and the great Powers drew up a declaration. "Napoleon," they said, "was an enemy to Europe; and, as a disturber of the peace of the world, must be treated as an outlaw."

"Ah, Wellington," said Alexander of Russia, "it is for you once more to save the world."

Ever since Napoleon had been at Elba, he had been in communication with the French. He heard of the unpopularity of Louis XVIII.; he knew that his own powers were not dead. Once more he determined to risk everything.

He made his preparations very secretly. He had a French ship painted in English colours at Naples, and brought round to Elba. Then one Sunday night, at nine o'clock, he quietly embarked with a thousand soldiers, on board the Inconstant. On doubling the island of Corsica, they fell in with a French cruiser. Its captain hailed the Inconstant and, hearing it came from Elba, asked how the Emperor was.

"He is marvellously well," answered Napoleon himself, ordering his soldiers to lie flat on deck to escape notice.

That danger was passed, and the little ship sailed on towards the coast of France.

"I shall reach Paris without firing a shot," prophesied Napoleon, as he stepped ashore near Cannes.

It was March 1, ten months since he had embarked for Elba. No force opposed his landing. A few days later, he issued the proclamation he had prepared.

"Soldiers," it ran, "we have not been beaten. In my exile I have heard your voice. I have arrived once more among you, despite all perils. Come and range yourself under the banner of your old chief."

He reached Grenoble in safety. But here was a crisis: Royalist troops barred the road. Amid a breathless silence, Napoleon advanced alone. He was a familiar figure, in his grey cloak and cocked hat.

"There he is! Fire on him!" cried a Royalist.

Not a shot was fired.

"Soldiers," cried a well-known voice, "if there is one among you, who wishes to kill his emperor, he can do so. Here I am."

Then the old shout, "Long live the Emperor!" burst forth on all sides as the soldiers, with tears running down their cheeks, flocked round Napoleon, vowing to be faithful again.

They were the soldiers of Louis XVIII.: they had refused to fire on Napoleon. The scene decided the fate of the expedition.

Soon Napoleon was at the head of 14,000 men, marching on Paris. On the evening of March 20 he entered the capital. Louis XVIII. had fled to Ghent that morning. As the well-known figure was recognised, a great shout arose, and as Napoleon stepped from his carriage, at the gates of the Tuileries, he was seized by French officers and carried up the grand staircase of the palace. It was for the fallen emperor "a moment of triumph, for which it was almost worth paying the price of Waterloo and St Helena."

For the next hundred days Napoleon ruled France once more. He had been gladly accepted by the French people, but rejected by Europe. With a marvellous courage, he now determined to march against Europe. And the four allies—Russia, Prussia, Austria, and England—prepared to march against France.

44

The Eve of Waterloo

"There was a sound of revelry by night,
And Belgium's capital had gather'd then
Her Beauty and her Chivalry, and bright
The lamps shone o'er fair women and brave men;

But hush! hark! a deep sound strikes like a rising knell!"
—BYRON.

Napoleon left Paris at daybreak on June 12.

"I go to measure myself with Wellington," he said as he stepped into his carriage.

The slumbering capital was soon left behind. In twelve hours he was at Laon. The weather was very hot. As he neared Belgium, the country stood thick with corn. The wheat was just flowering, the barley was nearly ripe, the rye stood shoulder high in the fields.

He pushed rapidly forwards. On the 14th he had reached his great French army, which awaited him near Charleroi, on the frontiers of France and Belgium. He mounted his charger. As he rode along the ranks a very storm of cheers greeted his arrival.

"Not so loud, my children," he exclaimed; "the enemy will hear you."

If the soldiers were proud of their commander, he had every reason to be proud of his army. It was composed entirely of Frenchmen, inspired with splendid fighting spirit. Before him stood heroes of Marengo, of Austerlitz, of Wagram—all with unbounded confidence in his leadership.

"Soldiers," ran Napoleon's proclamation, "to-day is the anniversary of Marengo, which decided the fate of Europe. For every Frenchman of spirit, the time is come to conquer or to die."

It was his last proclamation, as it was his last command.

For weeks past, the British and Prussian armies had been guarding the Belgian frontier from France, while huge hosts of Russians and Austrians were rolling slowly across Europe, to join them in a great invasion of France. Napoleon's plan was to march suddenly and directly upon Brussels, win over the Belgians to his cause, and thus plunge the Allies in a hostile country.

The distance from Charleroi to Brussels was about thirty-four miles. At a distance of some thirteen miles, lay the farmhouse of Quatre-Bras, at the crossing of four roads, as its name denotes; beyond it, some thirteen miles farther, was the village of Waterloo, eight miles from Brussels.

On June 15 Napoleon marched into the town of Charleroi, where he was joined by Marshal Ney. Wellington was in Brussels at the time, the headquarters of the British army. The town was crowded with English. Feasting and dancing went on every night. Napoleon was not expected yet awhile. The Duchess of Richmond was giving a ball on the night of the 15th. That very afternoon Wellington received the news of his movements. The great army of France, under its Emperor, was within thirty-four miles of the Belgian capital. Wellington ordered his troops to Quatre-Bras to hold the road to Brussels, and attended the ball to allay the fears of the English. Despatches reached him constantly during the evening. The situation was more dangerous than he thought. Officer after officer quietly left the ballroom at his command. At last he left too.

"Napoleon has humbugged me," he said to his host, the Duke of Richmond. "He has gained twenty-four hours' march on me."

"What do you intend to do?" asked the Duke.

"I have ordered the army to Quatre-Bras, but we shall not stop him there. I shall fight him here," said Wellington, putting his thumb over the position of Waterloo on a map, which the Duke had lent him.

Next morning, he was galloping in all haste to Quatre-Bras. There he found all quiet, and leaving the Prince of Orange in command, he hastened on to Ligny, some seven miles farther, where Blücher and a large army of Prussians were holding a position on the marshy banks of the stream running through the village of Ligny. Blücher had already drawn up his forces in battle array. From the window of a mill hard by, Blücher and Wellington watched the preparations of the French army. Together they arranged their plan of campaign against Napoleon.

But as he cantered back to his own ground at Quatre-Bras, he said to a fellow-officer, "The Prussians will make a gallant fight, for they are capital troops and well commanded: but they will be beaten."

Wellington reached Quatre-Bras to find that the fight was already beginning.

He had not arrived a moment too soon. With drums beating and shouts of "Long live the Emperor!" two French columns emerged from a neighbouring wood,—one moving off in the direction of Ligny, the other, under Marshal Ney, advancing on Quatre-Bras.

All through that summer afternoon, the two battles raged. Wellington and Ney fought amid the cornfields at Quatre-Bras, Napoleon and Blücher in the streets of Ligny, but a few miles distant.

The day had been hot and sultry. As the afternoon wore on, a terrible thunderstorm broke over the scene. Crash upon crash of thunder mingled with the booming of the guns, flashes of lightning lit up the darkness that had crept over the sun, and a deluge of rain washed the blood-stained earth. As the thunder-clouds rolled by, gleams of setting sun lit up the battlefields of Quatre-Bras and Ligny. Evening found Wellington still holding the position of the cross-roads, which Ney had failed to secure; it found Napoleon victorious over Blücher, and the Prussians in retreat towards Wavre, to the north-east.

The morning of the 17th broke. Wellington was riding along his outposts at Quatre-Bras by three o'clock in the morning. It was not till nine o'clock that he heard of Blücher's defeat and retreat.

"Old Blücher has had a good licking," he said. "He has gone eighteen miles to his rear: we must do the same. I suppose they'll say in England we have been licked. Well, I can't help that."

He then gave orders for the famous retreat to Waterloo.

Meanwhile Napoleon, knowing nothing of Ney's defeat at Quatre-Bras, slept late. He had driven away the Prussian army. He had now only the British under Wellington to destroy, and Brussels would be his.

It was not till the morning had passed, that Napoleon suddenly realised that the English were slipping away from him. Frantic that the foe should escape him, he drove hastily to Quatre-Bras. There he saw Marshal Ney.

"You have ruined France," he said angrily to him.

But it was the moment for deeds rather than words. He now gathered up his powerful cavalry and dashed after Wellington. It began to rain. Each hour the rain grew heavier, till the roads were ploughed up and the cornfields became impassable.

On raced the pursuers, on raced the pursued,—galloping for their lives through the storm. The Emperor rode at the head of his cavalry. He was drenched to the skin, his grey overcoat was streaming with wet, his hat was bent out of shape by the storm. It was not till darkness was falling that, on the ridge of Waterloo, Wellington stood at bay, and the truth was borne in on Napoleon, that his foes had escaped him that day.

Night fell, and still the rain poured down pitiless torrents. It was the eve of Waterloo.

45

Waterloo

"Waterloo did more than any other battle I know of
toward the true object of all battles—the peace of the world."
—WELLINGTON.

Sunday morning, the 18th of June, dawned grey and misty. The ground was sodden with the night's rain. Wellington was up early. He and Napoleon were face to face for the first time in their lives. Each must prepare for a tremendous conflict: each was confident of victory.

By six o'clock in the morning, the British troops and their allies were astir, a "miserable-looking set of men, covered with mud from head to foot," weary with the retreat of the day before. Mounted on his famous charger, Copenhagen, Wellington rode along the lines, as batteries, squadrons, and battalions took their appointed places, for the coming battle. His second in command asked him his plans for the day.

"Plans? I have no plans," answered Wellington impatiently, "except to give that fellow a good licking."

The road from Charleroi to Brussels ran across, and over, two ridges of hills, between which lay a narrow valley. On the top of the ridge, some nine miles from Brussels, Wellington posted his army. He had two advanced posts. One was on the road—the farmhouse of La Haye Sainte—under the command of the Prince of Orange and the Dutch allies; the other was Hougoumont, a farmhouse and castle strongly walled in, standing in the valley. On the ridge opposite, on the other side of the valley, the French army stood to arms.

"At last I have them—these English," said Napoleon.

"Sire," ventured Marshal Soult, who had fought against Wellington in Spain, "I know these English; they will die ere they quit the ground on which they stand."

"Bah!" was the answer. "You think that because Wellington defeated you, that he must be a great general. I tell you he is a bad general, and the English are bad troops: we will make a mouthful of them."

On his little white Arab, Marengo, Napoleon surveyed his troops with satisfaction, as with drums beating, colours flying, and bands playing they took up their position for the battle. He had intended to attack at nine o'clock; but he waited till the ground should dry, and it was half-past eleven before the first French guns rang out on the summer air.

The tremendous conflict of Waterloo had begun in deadly earnest.

Napoleon directed his first attack on Hougoumont, which, however, was held heroically, by British troops, throughout the whole of that long day. Early in the afternoon, the other outpost, La Haye Sainte, was taken by the French, and it seemed as if Napoleon would carry all before him.

Riding along his lines, Wellington encouraged his men.

"Stand fast," he urged; "we must not be beaten. What will they say in England?"

The French now approached the main line of the English, and so destructive was their fire, that the English squares broke and a gap was left in the centre.

It was a tremendous moment. Wellington himself led forward more troops to fill the gap. He was beset by questioning officers.

"There are no orders," he answered gravely; "only stand firm to the last man."

The French were gaining ground steadily, but more troops were wanted. Marshal Ney sent a message to the Emperor to this effect.

"More troops!" shouted Napoleon. "Where am to get them? Does he expect me to make them?"

It is impossible to do more, than mark the leading events of this eventful day. At half-past four Blücher and the Prussians arrived on the field. For fifteen long hours, the heroic leader of the Prussians, defeated and wounded though he had been, tramped over muddy roads to reach Waterloo, in time to fulfil his promise to Wellington. Napoleon saw them: still he did not despair. He sent another tremendous charge of French cavalry up the opposite ridge.

"Will these English never show us their backs?" he cried, straining his eyes through the smoke of the battle.

"I fear," said Soult, "they will be cut to pieces first."

It was past seven, and the battle was still undecided, when Napoleon prepared for his last final attack on the ridge of Waterloo.

"You shall sup at Brussels," he said confidently to the Imperial Guard, with whom he intrusted this final charge.

He watched their gallant ascent of the now slippery slopes, with triumph.

But suddenly Wellington's voice rang out clear above the storm of battle, "Up, Guards, and at 'em!"—such are the words that have passed into history—and from the shelter of the wayside banks behind the ridge, up rose the English Guards, 1500 strong. Like a very wall of scarlet, they reached the summit of the ridge and poured a withering volley into the French. It broke the French column, and soon the very flower of Napoleon's army was retreating down the hillside.

The Emperor was watching through his glass. Suddenly he turned deadly pale, and his hand fell to his side.

"Why, they are in confusion," he cried in a hollow voice. It was followed by a cry, almost a sob. "The Guard gives way!"

As the sun shot its last gleams over Waterloo, the supreme moment arrived. Wellington recognised it. Standing on the crest of the hill, his figure outlined against the bright western sky, he took off his cocked hat and waved it forward. It was the signal for a general advance. For nine hours his soldiers had patiently endured the fiery storm, and now they rushed in magnificent order down from the heights, in pursuit of the wildly retreating French.

Then Napoleon himself rushed into battle. He formed his Guards into four squares, and placed them across the line of retreat. The last stand of the French Imperial Guard, is one of the finest scenes in history. Like "fierce beasts of prey hemmed in by forest hunters," these men stood savagely at bay against their hosts of enemies. In vain, the British called on them to surrender.

"The Guard dies, and does not surrender," was the heroic answer. And they perished almost to a man.

Dusk was deepening into night, when Napoleon turned from the battlefield. "All is lost," he cried, as he turned his horse in the direction of Quatre-Bras. There he stopped, and looked yearningly toward Waterloo, while tears rolled down his pale cheeks. He had staked and lost all.

The victory was with the Allies; but it had been secured at tremendous cost. Both Wellington and Blücher together lost over 20,000 men.

Night was advanced, when Wellington, weary with the ten hours' fight, threw himself down to sleep at the little inn at Waterloo, his face still black with the dust and powder of the battle. Early in the morning, the doctor, at his request, brought the list of killed and wounded. He began to read it aloud to Wellington. He read for an hour; then he looked up. There sat the Iron Duke, his hands clasped together, while tears were making long white streaks down his battle-soiled cheeks.

"Go on," he groaned; "for God's sake go on. It is terrible."

So ended the battle of Waterloo. It ended the military careers of Wellington and Napoleon at the early ages of forty-six; it ended the great Napoleonic struggle, and brought to Europe thirty years of peace.

The Exile of St Helena

"He fought a thousand glorious wars,
And more than half the world was his;
And somewhere now, in yonder stars,
Can tell, mayhap, what greatness is."
—THACKERAY.

Napoleon arrived back in Paris at sunrise, on the 21st of June. It was but just over a week since he had left it, so full of hope and victory. Nothing was left to him now, but to abdicate a second time.

"Frenchmen," ran his proclamation, "I offer myself as a sacrifice to the hatred of the enemies of France. My political life is ended, and I proclaim my son Napoleon II., Emperor of the French."

But this was not allowed: he was ordered to leave France at once. Wellington and Blücher were already marching on Paris to restore Louis XVIII. once again. On July 7 they marched into the capital. The next day Louis arrived. Napoleon had reigned just one hundred days. To avoid arrest, he escaped to a seaport near La Rochelle, intending to sail for America. Here he was in sore straits, when the Allies bade him leave France within twenty-four hours. English ships were cruising in the Bay of Biscay. To put to sea ensured capture, to stay in France ensured arrest. He surrendered to the English captain of the Bellerophon. He wished to live in England, under an assumed name, as a private citizen.

"I come, like Themistocles," he said, "to seat myself at the hearth of the British people."

The Bellerophon sailed for England, and anchored at Plymouth for orders. Meanwhile the Allies had decided that the island of St Helena should be his home. It was a lonely island belonging to England, right away in the far Atlantic, midway between the coasts of Africa and South America. The vast waters, that rolled between France and St Helena would prevent any repetition of the escape from Elba, and British warships should watch the rocky coast of the island by day and night. No more could Napoleon upset the peace of Europe.

"I will not go to St Helena," he cried when he learned his fate. But in vain he protested.

"Better St Helena than Russia," said one.

"Russia! God keep me from that," he answered quickly.

On August 8, an English ship bore him away to St Helena. For the last time, Napoleon gazed at the dim coast of France, till it vanished from sight, and the great ship ploughed through the Atlantic waves, carrying the lonely exile to that far-off island, which was to be his prison and his grave.

It was October 16, when at last he stepped ashore. A guard of sentinels kept watch over him all day. Once in every twenty-four hours, a British officer had to see him, to make sure he had not escaped. All his letters were examined. He was addressed as General Bonaparte. The lord of so many palaces in Europe, was now confined to two small rooms. In the corner of one, stood his little camp-bed, with the green silk curtains, which he had used at Marengo and Austerlitz. On his walls hung a portrait of Maria Louisa, the wife who had shared his throne, but would not share his exile. A picture of his little son Napoleon, riding on a lamb, hung near him, and a miniature of Josephine, who not long survived his fall.

The days passed away in monotonous gloom. He read, he gardened, he drove out, he wrote an account of his deeds. Usually he was calm, but now and then he would burst forth about the past.

"It was a fine empire," he said one day. "I ruled eighty-three millions of human beings—more than half the population of Europe."

Six weary years slipped by.

Death came almost suddenly at the last. It was not till a week before the end, that either he or the doctors realised that the disease he had suffered from for years, was now killing him.

His mind went back to years that were past. "France," he muttered as he lay dying, "Army—Head of the army."

A great storm raged outside. It tore up the trees that Napoleon had planted, uprooted the willow under which he had sat, shook the frail tents of his sentinel soldiers; and "amid the tumult of the raging sea and the shaking land and the tempest-torn skies, the fierce spirit of Napoleon passed away."

Reverently they covered him with the martial cloak that, as a young conqueror, he had worn at the battle of Marengo. They buried him in the island of St Helena; but nineteen years later his body was taken back to France, and Paris, once his great capital, opened her arms to receive back her mighty dead. He who had raised her to such heights of glory, he who had dashed her to such depths of disaster, now lies in her midst.

The results of Napoleon's life were great and far-reaching. Not only had he re-moulded the France of the Revolution, but he had laid the foundations of new life in Italy and Germany. Everywhere in Europe, he had broken down the old barriers of custom and prejudice and created a new spirit of freedom and independence.

He had set his whole heart on the conquest of England, and in the end England had conquered him. She emerged from the long struggle "Clad with a great fame."

She had won the power of the sea. This was the secret of that success, that was to see her flag flying over a sixth part of the world in the century to come. But another secret was hers: she was firm in the belief of that watchword, which won for Nelson the battle of Trafalgar, for Wellington Waterloo; that watchword, which must ever lead her from strength to strength, as the years roll onward into space—"England expects every man to do his duty."

CPSIA information can be obtained at www.ICGtesting.com
Printed in the USA
BVOW08s1822240715

410096BV00003B/189/P